PRIMARY OBSESSIONS

Primary Obsessions

CHARLES DEMERS

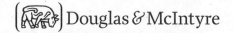 Douglas & McIntyre

Douglas and McIntyre (2013) Ltd.
P.O. Box 219, Madeira Park, BC, VON 2HO
www.douglas-mcintyre.com

Epigraph excerpted from Thomas Merton, *New Seeds of Contemplation,* Penguin Books Canada Ltd, 2007.
Edited by Caroline Skelton
Cover design by Anna Comfort O'Keeffe
Text design by Brianna Cerkiewicz
Printed and bound in Canada
Printed on 100 percent recycled paper

Douglas and McIntyre (2013) Ltd. acknowledges the support of the Canada Council for the Arts, the Government of Canada, and the Province of British Columbia through the BC Arts Council.

Library and Archives Canada Cataloguing in Publication

Title: Primary obsessions / Charles Demers.

Names: Demers, Charles, 1980- author.

Identifiers: Canadiana (print) 20200173138 | Canadiana (ebook) 20200173170 | ISBN 9781771622561 (softcover) | ISBN 9781771622578 (HTML)

Classification: LCC PS8607.E533 P75 2020 | DDC C813/.6—dc23

FOR M.R.

*Our minds are like crows. They pick up everything
that glitters, no matter how uncomfortable
our nests get with all that metal in them.*

Thomas Merton

1

"DO YOU WANT me to keep going?"

"I want you to move at whatever pace makes you feel comfortable. Don't worry about time."

"Okay. Well, then, like—I go to pull out the knife, but she's still breathing. And then every, like, breath she takes is—it's like kind of gasping? And it spatters, everywhere, blood. All over me, all over her."

"It's really important for me that you know that me asking about this, it's not about judgment."

"No, I know."

"I'm just trying to get a fuller picture."

"No, I know, I know," he said, and he was beginning to cry now, ignoring the box of tissues on the stand next to him, and instead wiping his eyes, his nose, all of it with the heel of his palm. "I just don't even like to say it out loud. Because..."

"It feels more real?"

"Yeah," he said, the waves breaking over the shore, his cheeks flooding with salty rivulets dully reflecting the soft lamplight in the room. The overhead fluorescents were off. They were always off. "I keep stabbing her and stabbing her, her eyes, her, like—her front. Like her, her down..."

"Her genitals?"

The young man nodded and sobbed.

"It's okay."

"It's not okay," he screamed quietly, grinding his teeth. "She's my mother. She's helpless. What kind of person does that to their own mother?"

During sessions like these, Dr. Annick Boudreau wished she still had her hair.

From her mid-teens, the impossible, untouched mane of thick, chestnut curls had been her trademark, the first thing about her. There had apparently once, in the kitchen at home, been a few snips underneath a metal bowl, an attempt by her father to trim the silken toddler locks falling down past her chubby cheeks before a family Christmas portrait, but otherwise, the hairs on her head had never been clipped, besides the routine eradication of split ends. When it hadn't been up in one of her elaborate braids, her hair had fallen right into her lap when she sat, and she could finger it imperceptibly while she listened to whomever was talking, pored over the details of their stories. But last spring, when her niece Marie-Élaine had begun chemotherapy, Annick had surprised her over the video chat with a cue ball—two shining Boudreau domes, one on the coast of the Pacific, one back home on the Atlantic. Now the crewcut was the first thing about Annick, which was fine—she had the cheekbones to carry the look, the dark eyes with lashes so long and thick they looked storebought—but at times like these, she didn't know what to do with her hands.

"Are you okay to continue, Sanjay?"

He nodded his head, biting back further tears. There was something still boyish about him; even in his mid-twenties, he hadn't fully grown into himself. His hands were large and long-fingered, with matching big feet, but his wrists were like a young woman's; he had a delicate chin, and downy sideburns not too far off of her own. He had shed none of his fragility since their first session, three months earlier.

"Obsessive-compulsive disorder comes from an error in interpretation," she explained, in language she used several times a day—outlining concepts that she had covered thousands of times before, with hundreds of patients, including Sanjay—always trying to find a margin of improvisation or interpretation within the parameters of what she had to get across, just to keep the moments alive. "These thoughts you're describing? Sanjay, everyone has them at one time or another. Everyone. They're standing at the bus stop, see a young mother holding her newborn, and for a split second they think, 'What if I pushed them underneath the bus?' So-called normal, regular people I'm talking about, now. Or sometimes it's the mother herself, she's all alone with her baby, and she thinks 'What if this child isn't safe with me?' or 'What if I did something sexually inappropriate to the baby?'"

Sanjay grimaced, disturbed; turning under the thought like a slug under salt.

"Jesus."

"Sure, him too."

"Sorry?"

"Well, sometimes I have religious patients, and they have horrible, for them, thoughts of blasphemy. Throwing the sacramental wine in the priest's eyes, or eating trayf if they're Jewish, hurling a Quran across the room. But these unwanted thoughts, whether they're of violence, or inappropriate sexuality, or blasphemy—the difference between someone with OCD and someone else isn't that they don't have these thoughts. It's that people without OCD know immediately that these thoughts are mental garbage. That they don't mean anything. But people with OCD make an error in interpretation—they think, 'I'm having these thoughts, so they must say something about me.'"

"Yeah, but I don't... I don't know."

"What don't you know?"

"Maybe everybody gets these thoughts, but I have them all the time. Doesn't that, I don't know—doesn't that mean something? Every time I close my eyes, right there on the back of my eyelids, she's there, it's my mom, and I'm cutting her throat, stabbing her—you know? That's so messed up."

"OCD is an anxiety disorder, and like any other anxiety disorder it comes from something like a short-circuit in the fight-or-flight instinct. So say we're back on the savannah..."

"My family's from northern India. There's no savannah." She appreciated the interruption; if he heckled, Sanjay kept Annick outside of the prepared script, the grooves worn into language by repetition. "Alright, you—we're all from Africa originally."

"Okay, okay, I'm sorry."

"We're on the savannah, and our minds and bodies know that we could be in danger, because of threats—panthers, tigers. Some kind of apex predator. Our minds and our bodies know that if there's a *lion* in the area, we're in big trouble. So for safety, for survival, we scan to ensure the absence of lions. But ironically, how do we establish that there are no lions?"

It took Sanjay a second to realize that the question wasn't rhetorical. "Huh? I don't know."

"What do we look *for*, in order to establish that there are no lions?"

"Lions?"

"Exactly. We confirm absence by scanning for presence. So similarly, when we're anxious, in present day, about a threat, we look for the threat. But when the threat is an intrusive thought, the only way to check for it is..."

"To think it?"

"You got it. So that's the error of interpretation. Rather than realizing that the thought is just garbage, people with

OCD worry that it means something about them. And to scan for the perceived danger that the thought represents, they keep having it."

"That's so fucked up," he said, not looking up at her anymore but instead at the carpet, his head shaking gently, gobsmacked at the sheer, galactic unfairness of it all.

"And the worst irony is, the people who worry the most about the thoughts are the people who are the most repelled by their contents. So the person who is constantly distressed by blasphemous thoughts? They're usually the most devout religious believer. And the people who have violent thoughts, they're actually the least likely to commit an act of violence."

"So you're saying no matter how often I have this image, this thought of killing my mother, I'm not a killer."

It was hard not to just give him what he wanted—to not reassure this young man who had first come to her after a May long weekend road trip, saying he'd nearly thrown himself off a trestle bridge in the Rockies to escape the murderous thoughts he couldn't stop himself from having. The young man with eyes red from tears now sitting across from her, his hands laid across knees he didn't even know were jackhammering.

"What do you think?" she asked instead.

"Please don't say that."

"No, really Sanjay. What do you think? Do you hate your mother?"

"I love her more than anything."

"What does that tell you?"

"I don't—I just need for you to tell me I'm not a killer."

Annick closed her eyes gently and inhaled.

"Look, I know it's not your job to—"

"It's not that it's not my job, Sanjay. It's that giving you reassurance may make you feel better in the short term, like the rituals of hand washing and repeating her name, but in the long run it reinforces the importance of the thoughts. Just like the compulsions do."

"But I'm not, right?" he asked again, his voice quavering just at the edges. "I just need to know that it's okay for me to be around her."

"Let me put it this way: If I thought you were a danger to your mother, or to yourself, or to anybody else, would I just let you go home at the end of the session?"

He chewed the inside of his cheek. "No, I guess not."

"Oh, you guess not. I'm glad my professional ethics are so firmly established in your mind."

He smiled.

"Alright, you—I'm going to see you next week. I want you to keep taking notes in your journal on the intensity and frequency of the thoughts. Let me know if there are any changes or shifts in the content, too."

"Got it," he said softly.

"Your hands look better than last time, the knuckles. So you're resisting the urge to wash them repeatedly?"

Sanjay shrugged, his face pursed with bitterness. "My asshole roommate was complaining about me using the bathroom too much and going through the soap so quick. He got all puffed up like he does, right up in my face. I didn't want to go through that with him again. It's just not worth it. I felt like I had to stop."

"Well, I don't know... sounds like he's doing you a favour. It's like with prostates—sometimes the gateway to good health is an asshole."

"Wow. Did you just come up with that?"

"Why do people find it so hard to believe that I'm spontaneously hilarious?"

"No, I didn't mean—"

14

"Sanjay, I'm joking."

"Anyway, I just—I know it's probably not good to follow up or whatever, but it's so hard. I'm just sitting there shaking, I just need to wash them. I feel like I'm going crazy if I don't, you know, do the thing with my hands under the water that, like..." He trailed off.

"That what, Sanjay?"

Sanjay murmured now, with a shame that was all too familiar in Dr. Boudreau's office: the shame of someone who knows something will sound crazy but has to say it anyway. "That cancels out the bad thoughts."

Annick nodded understandingly, with a smile that strove to be both warm and formal.

"I understand, Sanjay. And listen, it is very normal for people with primary obsessions OCD to have those kinds of external compulsions, as you might see in, say, movies about OCD... checking the stove, washing hands. And then there's the worst-case scenario, where the compulsions, and how they are or aren't carried out, can themselves become *evidence*—'I didn't lock the door because deep down I really want my husband to be hurt,' or 'I didn't wash my hands properly on purpose, because I want to hurt people.' It's a Chinese finger trap. You can't get out of it by pulling harder, because it just makes it worse. The only way, I promise you, to lessen the frequency of the thoughts is to lessen their power and importance. And for that, you're just going to have to sit with the anxiety you're describing. Know that it can't hurt you. That it can't last forever. Eventually, it goes away."

"Okay."

"Things are still tough with the roommate, huh?"

Sanjay rolled his eyes, shrugged, nodded, shook his head.

"That's quite the gamut of responses you just ran."

He smiled crookedly. "My mom's on me to move back in with her—I don't know. I'm thinking about doing it."

"Yeah?"

"Yeah. It's just that her place is so far from school. And I don't know—Jason's a dick, but beggars can't be choosers in this city, right? You find a room, you take it. The first time I met him I thought, you know—I mean the guy looks like a meathead. He is a meathead. But I don't know, he had all these old Vancouver hardcore posters up around the living room, nice frames and everything. Shows from before we were born, old D.O.A. shows from the Smilin' Buddha and stuff, and we talked about the Subhumans and the Modernettes. I thought, '*See?* Don't judge a book by its cover!' I don't think we ever talked about music again. I move in and he just goes straight asshole. I don't know. He's a bouncer, so at least I have the suite to myself at night. But when he's there..." Sanjay shook his head.

"No fun, huh?"

"These days I just stay in my room. If he's not fighting with his stripper girlfriend, or making up with her, which is even louder—he's out there on the couch with his idiot buddy. There was some new drama last week, some guy they'd bounced, and was he gonna be a problem, and blah blah blah."

"The friend is a bouncer too?"

Sanjay nodded. "They work the same club. I guess they laid into this guy pretty bad, then they found out he's all connected, owns these pubs and pizza places across the East Side..."

Annick shook her head. "It really sounds terrible, Sanjay."

"Yeah..." Sanjay said, his eyes finding the corners of the office, his face darting as though he were thinking about all of this for the first time.

"It might not be a bad idea to take your mom up on the offer. This sort of stress also turns the temperature up on your anxiety levels, and that can make OCD symptoms feel more intense."

Sanjay turned his palms upwards. "I know. For now, anyway, I've got the headphones."

"Okay—that works as a short-term solution, but it can't be the plan for the long haul. That sort of isolation, shutting the world out—sometimes that can exacerbate intrusive thoughts too."

"What doesn't?"

Annick laughed. "Fair question. Alright. I don't want you to do any reassurance-seeking behaviours with friends or with family, okay? And again, if you really can't sit with the thoughts, you can write them in your journal and we can look at them next time, alright?"

"Okay," he said, standing, the mask of confidence that he'd put on when discussing his roommate slipping visibly. He winced, though it wasn't clear at what.

"Alright. Sanjay," said Annick. "One time."

"Thank you."

"You are not a killer."

2

FOUR DAYS LATER, Annick Boudreau was staring with great resentment and intensity at the tall man looming in the doorway to her office.

"Remind me why I do these stupid things again?"

"Because you care about clinical practice?"

"No, I don't think that's it."

"Because you care about this clinic in particular?"

"No, not that, either."

"I would remind you that while a certain degree of aloofness is charming, Dr. Boudreau, you are at this point beginning to try my patience."

"Jesus, Cedric—if it means so much to you, why don't you go do it? That handsome face was built for television."

"I am well aware of my photogenic qualities, Annick. But I've got a group mindfulness session starting in half an hour."

Dr. Cedric Manley made up one hundred percent of the Jamaican-Canadian Zen Buddhist community in Vancouver, British Columbia, and he took those duties very much to heart. At just over six feet, he had a full submarine sandwich–length advantage in height over Annick, but his mostly raw vegan diet kept them at roughly the same weight. In her experience, though, if she could keep at least two-thirds of that weight confined to the right areas, she still got looks of approving curiosity from across the gender spectrum. So did he, she imagined.

"Fine, I'm going to do it, but I want you to put in a good word with the Buddha for me, bump that karma up a few notches."

"Good lord," Cedric said, shaking his head in understated disbelief. "Even your understanding of Buddhism is Catholic."

"Well, despite that," Annick said as she gathered up her travel mug and her purse and pushed past Cedric towards the door of the clinic, "I do not forgive you for this."

Annick's mug hissed and popped with diet cola as she slipped into the waiting cab outside of the West Coast Cognitive Behavioural Therapy Clinic, a soft and mossy-smelling summer rain breaking the muggy heat for a few merciful minutes.

"I'm headed to the CBC building downtown, please?" The cabbie nodded in the rear-view mirror, started the meter and Annick sipped her aspartame at a speed that would let her finish before arriving without leaving her gassy for her television appearance.

Cedric was convinced that appearing on news panels was good publicity for the clinic, and Annick reluctantly had to agree that it probably was. She also realized that between his being a tall, very handsome middle-aged man with a musical Caribbean lilt, and her being a short, very cute thirty-five-year-old woman with just the slight hint of an Acadian accent, it would always come down to one of the two of them for public appearances. It wasn't that their colleagues at the clinic were unpresentable—it was just that they all looked more or less exactly like what the words "cognitive behavioural therapist" conjured in the mind's eye.

But today's panel was not compelling. Dr. Annick Boudreau would be appearing alongside a local screenwriter to discuss the engineered controversy surrounding a newly released Hollywood gross-out comedy, a hollowed-out riff on the damaged genius formula called *One Cool DJ*. The cleverest thing about the movie, which was saying something, was that the first letter in each word of the title spelled *O-C-D*, referring to the neurotic qualities of the meticulously anal-retentive turntablist at the centre of what passed for its story, which involved a romantic infatuation with a deliberately offbeat and charmingly slovenly though pert love interest.

An online controversy had emerged (no doubt abetted by the film's publicity team) over whether or not the reference to OCD belittled and mystified an already poorly understood disorder. Two camps had emerged in response—one denouncing rampaging political correctness, and another bemoaning the insensitivity of the ableist privileged. As always, Annick mourned the fact that there was no third box to check, besides the ones marked "Callous Prick" or "Scandalized Hall Monitor."

Annick made her way into the CBC building through its beautiful glass and beam lobby, which had been installed just before a round of major funding cuts. She spoke to the bilingual security guard in French, a rare chance to practise her mother tongue in a city named for a British navy captain, and was beeped through the sliding security doors that brought guillotines to even the healthiest minds.

The anchor and moderator, Sam Gill, was an almost satirically good-looking South Asian man wearing perhaps the most perfectly tailored suit Annick had ever seen; her co-panellist, a rangy and not-bad-looking blonde, Cass Johannsen, had gone for the unkempt chic look preferred by the men of Vancouver's creative class, the sleeves of a

baby-blue linen shirt rolled up for maximum tattoo exposure. With some consternation, Annick realized that she was
wearing the charcoal pantsuit whose chief selling point was
the adorable package that it made of her bum; public broad-
caster or no, the cameras were unlikely to pan her ass. At
least not on the English-language side.

No sooner were polite nods exchanged and lavalier
microphones affixed to lapels than Gill launched into an
introduction that, predictably, set the table for a conversation built to produce lightless heat.

"Dr. Boudreau, do films like *One Cool DJ* make your
patients feel unsafe?"

"Unsafe!" Johannsen ejaculated caustically.

"Okay, Cass, we'll get to that. But I do want to hear from
Dr. Boudreau. Do movies like this make life more difficult for
your patients?"

"Well, Sam, to be honest I think my patients have other
stuff on their minds, most of the time."

"And yet, here you are," said Johannsen. When the cameras had gone on, her co-panellist's mien had changed
almost entirely, suggesting to her that he was in the midst
of a project of personal branding. He was asserting himself
as a professionally relaxed teller of things as they are. She
had seen it before.

"Well, I'm here because I was asked to speak to the general
public's understanding of obsessive-compulsive disorder,
and of the role that cultural industries play in that understanding. No, my patients don't wake up in the morning
or go to sleep at night thinking about crummy Hollywood
movies that nobody will remember in a year. More often,
they wake up, or go to bed, preoccupied with the unwanted
obsessions or tedious, time-consuming compulsions that
they're afflicted with."

The host, pinching his handsome face into a vague simu-lacrum of human seriousness, tried to interject. "So, then, if I'm hearing you right—"

"But yeah," Annick said, the last revs of the caffeine from her diet cola blasting out through her system, pushed to the brink of aggression by both the smug look on her know-nothing co-panellist's face and her simultaneous realization that she'd left her travel mug in the back of the cab. "When they're trying to express their disorders to the people in their lives, their loved ones, even themselves—it's inconvenient that the clinical term for what they're suffering has been belittled into a cutesy label meaning 'neat-freak.'"

"Now, Cass, you—"

"I mean, the people who make movies, I'm not sure they realize the power they're wielding when it comes to shaping public perceptions of an anxious condition that the general public knows virtually nothing about. For thirty years after *Rain Man*, everybody thought autism meant counting tooth-picks. Now they just think it means you've been inoculated against the mumps."

"I'm sorry, do I get to talk?"

"Go for it," Annick said, fully irritated now. "I'm willing to bet it won't be your first time today."

"Now, Dr. Boudreau, please."

"We can't have comedy without people getting offended."

"That's true."

"So you agree with me?"

"Yes, on a point unrelated to the conversation."

"But no, it's at the very heart of the conversation. You want to shut down a film because it doesn't toe your ideo-logical line."

"Wait, what film am I trying to shut down?"

"Dr. Boudreau, I'd like to ask—"

22

"Wait, no, sorry. What film am I trying to shut down?"

The screenwriter rolled his eyes. "You want this movie to fail simply because—"

"Listen, my friend, I don't care one way or the other what happens to this movie. To be honest, just the fact that it's not about superheroes kind of has me rooting for it."

"But to call for a boycott—"

"Boycott? I'm just saying your movie doesn't give an accurate—"

"Well it's not my movie," he huffed.

"What?"

"I didn't write the movie," Johannsen said peevishly, clearly unhappy to have been forced to break his affectation of studied chill.

"Wait, sorry—if it's not your movie, then what are you doing here?"

"Unfortunately that's all the time we have, I'd love to have you both back to discuss this anytime. I want to thank our guests, local screenwriter Cass Johannsen..."

"Thanks for having me," he said curtly.

"And Dr. Annick Boudreau..."

"You know who would be great next time is my colleague Cedric."

~

As she made her way back out through the newsroom, Annick frowned as she looked into the adorably cluttered cubicle next to a load-bearing concrete pillar and found it empty. As she craned her neck, climbing to the tips of her toes to take in what she could of the open office, she felt a series of undulating fingers working their way down the small of her back.

"Jesus, does your ass look incredible."

"I knew I wore this suit for a reason."

Annick leaned over to plant a kiss on her boyfriend's lips. Philip Lee, a science journalist who had somehow dodged round after round of layoffs with all the luck and aplomb of a baby sea turtle scuttering to the water's edge, now ran his fingertips gingerly down the sides of Annick's thighs, and instantly erased the taste left in her mouth by the panel.

"I was hoping you'd still be here."

"Well, the effects on genome patenting from the new free trade deal with the Kingdom of Jordan aren't going to sort themselves on their own."

"That was about one hundred pounds of content in a twenty-pound sentence."

"I know, I lost the thread of it myself halfway through."

"Well clearly you don't have any work left in you. Let's walk home? I came in a cab."

"Oh, memories. I remember that time."

"You are disgusting."

"Listen, you head home, I've got another hour here, but that's tops. We'll reheat the rest of that lasagna from Tuesday."

"It is so cute that you think I didn't already eat that lasagna."

"Phil?" It was a smoky, well-calibrated voice coming from behind Annick's shoulder, an alto shot through with terrific confidence. Annick turned to see a tall, handsome woman in a very expensive suit that wasn't supposed to look like one. "I'm sorry to interrupt."

"No, no problem, Bonnie," said Phil, standing. "Bonnie, have you met my girlfriend? Dr. Annick Boudreau."

Annick smiled and stuck out her hand. "He always says 'doctor' in case one of his scientist pals thinks I'm just a dumb girl." Bonnie gave a small smile, and shook hands.

"Actually, we met at the Christmas party last year. You came to my rescue."

"How's that?" Bonnie arched an eyebrow.

"When I was cornered by the guy from the cooking show?"

A slow and subtle smile began to spread across Annick's face. "I have only hazy recollections of this..."

"You interrupted him talking at me, and said 'Hey, check out the face on that pair of tits.'"

Bonnie made an unsuccessful attempt at suppressing her pride.

"Okay, I remember now."

"His neck snapped up so quickly I thought he was going to have to wear a brace."

"Sure, or an electric collar."

"It's wonderful to have all of these strong women in my life," said Philip, "but a little terrifying when they get together like this. What can I help you with, Bonnie?"

"They told me you were promised the J-school placement kid this evening?"

"Lindsay? Yeah, she's going to help me scan this trade deal for keywords."

"Any chance it could wait?"

"Well—I could probably make do on my own. You need her?"

Bonnie nodded with an urgency all out of sync with her bearing and her outfit. "I'm supposed to be doing some fact-checking calls on that smuggling story with the lumber port on the island, but we just had a real blood and guts story come in. I have to go."

"Oh, no," said Annick.

"Of course, Bonnie," said Philip.

"Yeah, young guy in Kitsilano, upstairs landlords heard screaming and called the police. They found him with his throat opened up, his roommate in the bathroom calmly washing up after. I gotta get over to VPD."

"Jesus."

"Christ. Yeah, of course. I can handle this on my own."

"Thanks, Phil. Annick, nice to see you." Bonnie nodded and left, and Philip let out a long, frustrated exhalation as he planted himself in his seat.

"You better grab your own dinner."

"My God, what are you, made of stone?"

"What?"

"Some kid gets gutted and you want to talk about dinner?"

"It's a newsroom, Annick—what are we supposed to do? Every day it's something like this. You know how it is, you hear this stuff all day long."

"I most certainly do not."

"Whatever, you know what I mean. You've gotta defend yourself against taking it all on too intimately, caring too much. Get some sushi, okay? And leave me some? Farmed salmon."

"For fuck's sake, Phil, I'm not getting farmed salmon. You're a scientist, you should know better."

"I prefer the taste of farmed salmon. It's Atlantic, and it's got just the right amount of fat. Like Acadian tail," he said, pinching the back of her pants. She smacked the back of his head, then leaned down and kissed him on the temple. As she stood, she scanned the newsroom again, shaking her head.

"I don't know how you guys do this. It would kill me."

"You'd survive."

3

"DID YOU HAPPEN to catch the news last night?" she heard, the exaggeratedly singsong Jamaican accent stopping her as she tried to make it to her office unnoticed. Annick cringed.

"Please don't start, Cedric," she said, putting on convincing airs that she was in the midst of a particularly difficult morning. Cedric was standing now at the door to his office—no one had ever successfully arrived earlier than him, and there was no empirical proof that he ever went home—with a condescending smile. He loomed over Annick like a beautiful sunrise, invisibly firing carcinogenic UV rays.

"You know, cognitive behavioural therapy is very different from talk therapy—but the viewing audience certainly wouldn't have known that yesterday evening."

Annick smiled. "You've got me all wrong, Dr. Manley. My approach yesterday was purely Freudian—I was showing that screenwriter that mine was bigger than his."

It was no easy thing to send a ripple of shock and surprise across Cedric's implacable Zen features, but she had managed to score an unambiguous point.

"Alright then, whatever's in that coffee, I want some—it's working," he said, deadpan. "I'll take the next few panels."

"You know, the whole time I was on TV I kept thinking to myself, 'If being here gets through to just one person, convinces just *one* of my colleagues that he should be doing these things instead of me, it'll all be worth it.'"

"However," Cedric said, ignoring her joke with exaggerated dignity, "this does not absolve you of your public relations responsibilities in their entirety. We still need the new pamphlets taken care of, with the proper website information and the group programs."

"Say no more. New pamphlet duty for no more TV or radio spots, that's a steal in my book."

"'No more' might be putting it just a touch strongly. No more *for now*."

"You know, for a Zen master, you can be very ominous."

"Even Buddhists have limits. Shall we celebrate the arrangement with lunch, then? The Thai place?"

"Actually, can we rain check? I have a lunch date—Philip has the morning off, so he's bringing sandwiches to the park up the block."

"He's a lovesick fool."

"Absolutely hopeless case. You can't reach some people— they're just fucking nuts."

Annick sat at her desk and went over notes from the last session with her next patient, the deeply depressed Catherine, but she found her mind wandering to thoughts of Sanjay. Over the years, Annick had gotten used to the fact that some patients got under one's skin more than others; burrowed in and made their suffering one's own. There was also the fact of his youth—not so much that it made him boyish and sympathetic, although there was that, but that she really had the chance, if they could crack his case together, of giving him back the next fifty years. Catherine, who would be here soon, was in her mid-sixties, and though of course she was entitled to just as much sympathy, just as much help, there was part of Annick that realized that their work together would always be maintenance. It was unlikely that someone who had suffered from depression or anxiety on and off for half a century would ever completely shake either of them; by middle age, the game was survival, and God knows that was no mean thing. But Sanjay was barely through life's overture; he was just about to get started. Annick could do exponentially more for him. She could save his life.

After Catherine with depression at ten and Benson with panic attacks at eleven, it was suddenly noon, and Philip, who had used his free morning to full advantage, showed up with sandwiches, an adorable haircut and a brand new travel mug filled with caffeinated reinforcements just in time to ward off a midday headache.

"What'd I ever do to deserve you?" asked Annick.

"You really want me to remind you what you did? In public?"

In the wake of the previous day's rain, Vancouver had gone back to baking, with a smell that was not quite good but not quite bad, like a fruit-laden brie. The park was a welcome respite. At this point in the year, the grass had not yet turned brown. The city was built on top of a temperate rainforest, but the mountaintop winter snows and spring melts had decreased with the rising temperatures, leaving a town that had been granted a natural abundance of water bone-dry for long stretches of summer. The couple chose a bench accented with both the least and least fresh bird droppings. Philip produced a pair of simple brisket on focaccia sandwiches with spicy mustard and sprouts. He pulled two cans of cold brew coffee, still icy and wet with condensation, out of the bag, and handed one to Annick. She put it down next to the half-empty travel mug.

Annick took a bite of her sandwich, grabbed Philip's forearm and moaned.

"That good, huh?"

"See, farmed beef I have absolutely no problem with." They sat and chewed in a silence of easy intimacy, and Annick watched as a pair of seagulls pecked and screeched at each other over the remaining parts of a discarded bagel.

"What happened with that story last night? The murder?"

"Sad case," Philip said after swallowing. "Like Bonnie said, some kid murdered his roommate."

"Oh," Annick said, immediately regretting that she'd brought it up, and mourning the lighthearted sexiness of the lunch date, now departed. "Wait, a kid? With a roommate?"

"Young man in his twenties. The upstairs neighbours, I guess the landlords, heard a scream from the basement, called the cops. The victim was slashed across the throat, and they found the roommate in the bathroom wearing noise-cancelling headphones, giving his hands and forearms an industrial scrubbing. Creepy as shit."

"Oh, God that's awful," she said. And then: "Wait..."

"Yeah, it's brutal. The cops say they searched the roommate's room, and right out on the desk is this journal full of just, like, the most insanely violent imagery, stabbings, throat-slashings. The kid's a psycho. Bonnie said the VPD sergeant, some guy named Bremner, he was practically on the verge of cracking jokes at the press conference, he was so cocky. Had a look on his face like he'd just sunk a three-pointer."

The bottom of Annick's stomach somehow fell out from underneath her at the very same instant it leapt into the back of her throat. She stopped herself because it couldn't be right; it couldn't. It was too big a city for that; it couldn't be him.

Furthermore, patients with primary obsessions OCD never did it—they never, statistically, *never* acted on their thoughts. That statistic, that fact, was one of her most powerful therapeutic weapons, marshalled constantly to remind her suffering charges that there was no inherent link between thought and action, that there was no chance that they would snap under the pressure one day and actually do any of the horrible things that they were constantly forced to imagine.

And yet, even knowing that, her mouth was so dry that she felt it might pull her lips, her whole face, in, and she took a swig of the cold brew coffee and felt it pour directly into her chest cavity, the centre of which was now pumping toxically and arrhythmically.

"Love, you okay?"

"I'm fine, just some sandwich went down the wrong pipe. I'm great. This sandwich... this sandwich is so good."

Philip smiled; he'd gotten all the reassurance he needed. "I knew I'd found my soulmate when you told me you liked simple sandwiches. All that mayo, nine different vegetables— what are they trying to hide, man?"

"Sweetie, the suspect, in the murder?"

"I don't think he's a suspect, Annick. It's pretty open and shut."

"Did they—do they have a name?"

Philip furrowed his brow as he reached for his phone. "It's something Indian," he said, and Annick's pounding heart seemed to stop as he scrolled through his newsfeed. "'Police have arrested a suspect, Sanjay Desai, twenty-five...'"

Annick didn't hear the end of the sentence.

4

SHE HAD NO recollection whatsoever of walking the two blocks back to the office; no sense of whether or not she had kissed Philip goodbye, or how she had hidden from him the secret of her patient's identity. If her fallen face, her slackened jaw, her swimming eyes had signalled anything, Philip knew her well enough not to pry into the ethical space that she reserved for her and her patients—she was a doctor as a first principle, and there were no personal intimacies that superseded that code. As a scientist, that was part of what Philip had fallen in love with.

When she came out of the fog, she was sitting at the desk inside of her locked office, her hand trembling over the mouse pad. She grabbed the mouse and shook her sleeping screen to life. Annick looked up at the wall clock and tried, and failed, to do the simple arithmetic necessary to determine how long it was before her next patient came in. She turned away from the computer, locking her eyes on the clock, and tried, again, to count the minutes. She had to use her fingers before she could be sure. She had fourteen minutes.

She leapt up out of her seat before having decided to, before having figured out what use she could be standing that she couldn't be sitting down. If there was anything, she couldn't think of it, so she sat back down in the seat closest to her, which was, this time, the chair she reserved for patients. The chair where Sanjay had been sitting just five days ago. The chair from which he had stood up before hearing her promise. He was not a killer.

Eleven minutes.

There were eleven minutes until another patient would come in through the door, a patient who needed her just as much as Sanjay did. But that was bullshit, wasn't it? Sanjay was in jail, perhaps by now at the pre-trial centre, facing what would be, in all practical likelihood, the end of his life as a free man.

Nine minutes.

Annick thought of Cedric's constant tips for attaining mindful calm, delivered promiscuously to patients and to colleagues, desperate people as well as those who hadn't asked for advice. She tried to mimic his centred breathing, the calming embodiment of mindful consciousness that he taught to his anxiety patients; she tried to count her breaths.

In, one. Out, one.

In, two. Out, two.

In, three.

Fuck, this.

Bull, shit.

Eight minutes.

Annick sprang back up and stood at the computer. If Sanjay had spoken to a lawyer, which was likely by now, the lawyer almost certainly would have explained how confidentiality works in cases like these: there was nothing much that they could make Annick do, but nothing much that she could do, either, without Sanjay waiving his rights and bringing her in. But if she got to say anything, they could make her say everything; subpoena her notes, all of it.

If the journal of Sanjay's intrusive thoughts was being used as a key piece of evidence, it was likely that both Crown and defence counsel would want to bring her in as a witness eventually, but both sides had every reason to play cat and mouse about it. The Crown could suspect that her testimony would actually hurt their case; that there was a perfectly benign, therapeutic reason for the grisly diary, which, of course, there was. The defence, for their part, could spring a trap for the Crown: let the prosecuting attorneys request a look at the psychological evidence, and then, when inevitably they didn't use it, hold that up as proof that they'd seen the evidence and decided that it exonerated the accused.

Four minutes until her next patient arrived. Annick thumped her toes on the floor as though the answer to her problem had to be shaken up out of her feet. She shook her head. There was nothing that she could do in four minutes. Nothing beyond running to the window, sliding it wide open and screaming, '*He didn't do it!*' out towards Cambie Street.

But what if he had?

Annick felt the wind go out of her, and she sat back down in her own seat as her head began to swim. The thought hadn't occurred to her, until now, that this could have been anything but a mistake. But—

There was a hard rap at her door, and Annick's first impulse was to hide from it. She wanted badly to pretend that she hadn't heard it, until the circumstances snapped back into focus. She took a deep, long breath, without counting; she stood, unbuttoned and then rebuttoned her lightweight summer suit jacket. She used her hands to straighten her hair before remembering once again that she didn't have any, and strode to the door. When she opened it, she saw her one o'clock patient, a man about her own age with generalized anxiety disorder whom she'd been seeing clinically for just over a year.

"Dr. Boudreau? I am so, so sorry, but I didn't have any change for the meter—your receptionist very kindly broke my five for some coins. Is it okay if I just quickly run up the street to feed the meter?"

"Yes!" she nearly screamed, which is not the preferred mode of communication for those suffering from generalized anxiety disorder, and her patient winced accordingly. "I'm so sorry, Paul. I'm sorry. It's absolutely fine. Please go feed the meter. I'll be right here."

"Okay. Thank you," answered Paul with some trepidation, before taking off at a trot, the coins jiggling in his shorts pockets.

Annick slumped down onto the floor, her back against the door. Four minutes had nothing to do with it; for the time being, there was nothing she could do, full stop. Even reaching out directly to Sanjay could endanger his right to keep his treatment confidential—she would have to wait until he got ahold of her, as his counsel would ultimately, inevitably, do.

Unless.

Annick pinched the bridge of her nose and spread the fingers hard under her eyes in an utterly futile massage. She thought of Sanjay, held together by nerves, shame and guilt, thought about the progress or lack of it that they had made over the twelve weeks they'd been seeing each other. He was a bright kid, no question, and he didn't have a stitch of trouble understanding something conceptually, analytically or rationally.

But OCD didn't come down to analysis or rationale. Primary obsessions was a disorder with all of the violent magical realism of a Colombian crime novel—a place where the rules of the world as it is were only in effect right up until the second that they weren't; a place like the internet, where evidence was considered, but without perspective or scale. Sanjay understood how OCD worked, but he didn't *know* that he had it. This was the dance with a huge number of patients at the beginning, often for months: their abiding belief in their own demonic nature outweighed any number of framed degrees, diplomas and certificates on the wall. *You might be right about other people*, they thought, *but you've never come across a case as special as mine before.* She understood that, viscerally, Sanjay still thought that whatever might be the case with her other patients he, Sanjay Desai, had these unceasing, blood-soaked thoughts because he was a monster.

Annick and Philip had watched a movie, once, about the East German secret police, in which one Stasi officer had remarked to an underling that an innocent person, falsely accused, will respond with rage. Most people were convinced they weren't villains, and in the event that they were accused of some monstrosity, they could count on their enraged dissonance, the knowledge that they had been wronged, to fuel their defence.

But people with primary obsessional OCD were different. People like Sanjay spent all of their time worrying that they were getting away with something terrible, unspeakable. They were convinced that they were ghouls, the most vicious beasts on the planet, and that no one was holding them to account. That they represented an unchecked danger to those around them. Robert Frost once said that a liberal was a man too broad-minded to take his own side in a quarrel; Dr. Boudreau's patients were men and women too convinced of their evil to take their own side in a trial. Annick's hands sank to the floor as she considered the possibility that Sanjay might be too far gone in his mania for self-prosecution to fight for his own freedom. Maybe he wouldn't tell the lawyer anything.

Or, maybe he had killed his roommate.

The idea felt like tripping on something, and Annick struggled to catch her breath.

She opened the door to her office, her legs wobbling underneath her as she walked down the corridor to Cedric's. She leaned herself against the frame of his open door, half to keep from falling.

"Cedric?"

"Ah, the new face of mental health. What can I do for you?"

"Cedric," she started again, unsure of exactly what she planned to ask. Sensing that his flip greeting hadn't been properly tuned to his colleague's mood, Dr. Manley snapped into solemnity, picking his glasses up from the desk and replacing them on his face.

"Annick? Are you okay?"

"No, yeah. Fine. I just—I wanted to ask..."

"Sit down."

"No, no thank you, Cedric. I have a patient coming in. I—I just..."

Cedric's face fell into a groove of pure paternal comfort and shepherding concern.

"It's nothing, I just wanted to know—in your practice, or in your research, have you ever come across..." Annick searched for the words that would best keep Sanjay's confidentiality intact. "Do you know what the numbers are on primary obsessional OCD and violent crime?"

"Pardon?" Cedric's face wrinkled as though she'd asked the rabbi for a lobster recipe. The question was not only crazy; it was a violation of an understanding that they shared explicitly. "I don't understand what you're asking, Annick. You know that it's zero—"

"No, I don't mean acting on the content of their thoughts, I mean in unrelated violent crime. Not, like, the things from the intrusive thoughts—other violence."

Cedric shook his head incredulously. "I can't—I don't know that that research exists. Whence would the data be extracted?"

Cedric's use of *whence* in a spoken sentence worked on Annick in the manner of a gentle pinch, and brought her back to reality. She was doing it—this was reassurance-seeking behaviour.

"You're right. I'm sorry. Never mind."

"Dr. Boudreau?" it was Paul, standing tentatively behind her.

Annick took a deep breath and turned, trying to centre herself. Sanjay hadn't killed anyone, and they would certainly figure that out soon enough. There was nothing she could do for Sanjay this afternoon, and certainly nothing that she could do during Paul's session. Paul had a right to her undivided attention, and she had a responsibility to her other patients. Annick returned Paul's smile, then turned back towards her colleague.

"Sorry, Cedric. Just ignore what I said."

She pivoted to Paul again, still smiling, and walked back with him to her office. Annick closed the door, sat down across from her patient, then leaned back and turned off the computer monitor.

"So?" she asked, eyebrows folding up into her most empathetic listening expression. "What's going on? How have you been doing?"

"Yeah," said Paul, moving his head in a motion that was just as much shaking as nodding. "I don't know. It's been a pretty anxious time."

"Yeah? Tell me about it."

5

"YOU KNOW THAT I was joking, right? I had no expectation whatsoever that you would actually come?"

"I couldn't sleep anyway. And I have some stuff to wrap my head around—is that why you people do this? To clear your heads?"

"'You people'?"

"I'm sorry, I didn't—"

"Annick, chill. I was joking. You're not capable of offending me in my capacity as part of the running community."

"Sorry," she smiled meekly, embarrassed. "I'm just so sick of Jogging-Canadians on the whole, you know? Taking our jobs, marrying our men."

"Hey, our taxes pay for your elevators, even though we take the stairs."

"Okay, now I'm starting to get the feeling that you've actually thought about all this."

Philip smiled, pulling his foot up behind the small of his back, readying himself for a run along the seawall which was filling, even this early in the morning, with foot and bicycle traffic, and the beginnings of the day's heat. From wireless earbuds to gel insoles, his lithe, medium-height body was branded with all the markings of Vancouver's professional-managerial fitness cult. In his sleeveless shirt, the inky remnants of a few misspent teenage years on the wrong side of the law were the only thing off-brand from the West Coast yuppy aesthetic, but those tattoos were also the only part of the ensemble sexy enough that Annick had repeatedly, over the years, been willing to engage in a sweaty post-jog tackle.

The other women sprinting past them in front of the jade green waters and bright blue mountains of Coal Harbour were wearing yoga pants that operated upon the human ass with the same flaw-obliterating effects as Photoshop, and sports bras as supportive as a loving spouse. Annick understood that there was a vague cultural obligation for her to be envious, to be jealous of her beautiful boyfriend sharing his morning exertions with these beautiful women, but as she watched them bounce past all she could think about was how nice it would have been to sleep for another forty-five minutes.

Philip dropped his warm-up for a second and took Annick's shoulder in his hand. "Listen, are you okay?"

"Yeah, yes. Why do you ask? I'm fine."

"Wow, what a perfectly human syntax—I can't believe I thought anything was wrong."

"Okay, I'm sorry."

"I feel like yesterday, at lunch, something started bugging you. You hardly said anything last night at dinner or sitting in front of the TV, and suddenly this morning you want to go for a run for the first time since grade nine PE. What's going on?"

Annick wrapped her arms around the trunk of Philip's torso, squeezed him tight, then let go. She tilted up to face him, and shook her head.

"I need you to trust me that anything that's bothering me that I'm allowed to talk to you about, I will. And then, when I can't, I need you to let me sort through things on my own."

"That's like a Buddhist koan or something."

"No, love—it's like a professional ethical commitment or something."

Philip nodded his head, and leaned down to kiss her on the mouth, eyes and forehead.

"I get it."

"I know you do."

"You're a good doctor."

"No, I'm not. I'm really, really an excellent doctor."

"Sorry, I misspoke."

"It's okay. I know how you people are."

"You ready to go?"

"I think I got it out of my system."

Annick kissed Philip again, and left the seawall to him and the rest of the Lycra-clad Grecian gods who jogged with the fervent certainty that neither Death nor Ugliness would ever come.

~

Even after the abortive attempt at running, the trip back to the condominium for a shower and the change of clothes, Annick still arrived at the clinic before anybody else—even Cedric, who was now confirmed as being a bona fide human being, with a biological need for sleep, hearth and home. Putting her store-bought cappuccino down on the office kitchen counter, Annick prepared the first urn of collective coffee, though the office was ideologically riven by conflicting views as to caffeine's role in exacerbating anxiety disorders. The tea-drinkers could be entombed with their precious rooibos and peppermint, for all she cared.

Annick sat at her desk and went over the three months' worth of notes she'd taken on Sanjay, trying to get an ordered sense of the young man to set against the news stories. She frowned when she realized how many times the roommate had come up, always in a negative light. There had been embarrassed stories about getting caught mid-compulsion by the roommate's walking in unannounced; fights over noise; arguments about the use of common spaces, including the bathroom. The picture of the now-murdered Jason was uncomplimentary: thuggish, lazy, sleeping well into the day and noisily inhabiting the night when he wasn't busy as the doorman at a downtown club. There was a dim-witted and loutish friend, Mike, who seemed to be inseparable from the roommate and who was just as bad, if not as smart. But there had not been a single instance of Sanjay's even imagining visiting violence upon Jason. Did that make things better or worse?

"Pardon me."

Annick turned to see Cedric leaning the top half of his body through her open door. "Dr. Boudreau, a man's got a certain reputation to maintain. Imagine my surprise coming in with no alarm beeping, and instead hearing the mellifluous sound of percolation from the kitchen."

"Could've been worse—could've been one of our tea-crusader friends."

"I believe the preferred term is 'tea bags.'"

"Gotcha."

"You are feeling okay, Annick?"

"Sure, Cedric. Why do you ask?"

"Well, I was thinking of your question yesterday, so speedily retracted—and on top of that, you have a certain... underslept quality about you this morning."

"You certainly know how to make a lady feel special."

"Well, as your friend and colleague, I'm not so deeply concerned with making you feel special, Doctor. I want to make sure you're alright."

Annick smiled without happiness, nodded, shrugged. "Just a patient, has me worried is all."

"The only thing more painful than being good at your job is caring about it, too. Anything I can help with?"

"I can't see how, Cedric, but if I think of anything, I'll come to you."

"And I'll be there when you do," he said, turning to leave.

"Thanks, Cedric," she called out after him.

"Oh, and if anybody asks," he called back, over his shoulder, "I was in my office when you got here this morning."

Annick smiled and began to formulate a comeback when her computer *dinged* at her, and she turned to discover an email.

From: Dr. Supriya Desai
Subject: my son

6

FOR LUNCH, ANNICK had two cans of Diet Coke and six miniature Peppermint Patties—a jar of which sat ready for patients and colleagues to take from. Since they rarely did, she usually cycled through them all by herself every three or four months. Assured that her body was fortified with artificial sugar substitutes and edible wax, she once again pored over the email from Sanjay's mother.

Dear Dr. Boudreau—

My son Sanjay has asked me to reach out on his behalf in order to dialogue with you. He says that you have been instrumental in helping him to deal with his recent depression, and for this we are both truly grateful. As you have no doubt by this time been made aware, by sundry sensational media accounts, my child has been arrested for the murder of his odious roommate, Jason MacGregor, although he is entirely innocent of these charges—but of course, you know this, having spoken with him in such depth and detail that you must surely be aware that he is incapable of any such thing. Sanjay may also have indicated in his sessions with you that a great deal of my poetic practice has addressed the liminal conjunctures between street and state violence(s), and as such I am afraid that there may be a revanchism shaping the police treatment of his case in retaliation to my anti-brutality cultural engagement. They have told Sanjay that he is being held as a continuing danger because of a so-called "murder journal" filled with the most grotesque, baroque, violent imagery, which is melodramatic nonsense, of course. As his counsel have advised against an official meeting between the two of you at this time, Sanjay has asked me instead to meet with you in person, in order to relay from him the details of his case. He was very emphatic upon the point; he indicated to me the absolute importance that I convey his innocence to you. He is currently being held at the Dunsmuir Jail on Cordova, in the Downtown Eastside, and since I am not always permitted to have my phone with me there, or have sometimes been asked to turn off the ringer, it's perhaps best that we communicate today by email. Please let me know, urgently, your very earliest convenience for a meeting, preferably this evening, and I will endeavour to make my way to you.

Supriya
****

Dr. Supriya Desai, Ph.D.
Associate Professor
Department of English
Simon Fraser University
Unceded Musqueam, Squamish, Tsleil-Waututh, and Kwikwetlem territories
she/her/hers

Annick sat back from where she had been hunched towards the screen and let out a long, strong and resigned exhalation. Sanjay was still hiding his OCD from his mother. Given that she was the very subject of the great majority of Sanjay's dark and violent, unwanted and intrusive thoughts, maybe that was no particular surprise. He had never said as much, but Annick had begun to suspect that one of the reasons he had moved across town was to avoid the constant contact with his mother, who had no idea that she was being gutted in his mind's eye, against his will, for the longest hours of the day.

So Sanjay hadn't told his mother, and that would make things harder for everyone. Annick couldn't divulge any details about their sessions without Sanjay's direct permission. She couldn't explain primary obsessions OCD, or why a doctor might ask a patient to keep a record of the frequency, intensity and even content of intrusive thoughts—a record that, for someone who didn't know what they were looking at, might read like Dostoevsky by way of Charles Manson. Politically, Annick was more or less inclined to agree with Dr. Desai's diagnosis of the brutal biases and even vindictiveness of the constabulary, but this seemed like a simple case of convenience: that piece of evidence—a chronicle of imagined killings at the site of a real one—would make all the cops' and lawyers' lives easier. Everybody's lives, that is, but Sanjay's.

Annick had written an email full of solidarity and attestations to Sanjay's decency that were as vague as they were sincere. She'd suggested that the two of them might meet at a Palestinian restaurant on Hastings, not too far from the jail but far enough to be removed, since they'd probably both need something substantial to eat by then, and since the owners were friends of Annick's they could count on a table with some privacy. Supriya had written a very short email back, in the affirmative. They'd take a late dinner tonight, at eight o'clock.

There were lamb, chickpeas and eggplant in her future, but for the next seven and a half hours, a half-dozen peppermint chocolates dissolving in an acid bath of diet cola would have to do. She had twenty minutes left until her one o'clock patient, and that time wouldn't be taken up with anything as pedestrian or self-sustaining as, say, heading to the sub-par coffee franchise in the lobby of the building for a triangle samosa wrapped, for reasons that weren't immediately apparent from an ethnocultural standpoint, in a spinach tortilla.

Instead, she would spend her remaining moments of leisure and replenishment going back over the session notes about Jason MacGregor—Jason, whom Sanjay hadn't liked at all, but whom Supriya, it seems, found not just unlikable but "odious."

But the notes weren't any different than they had been in the morning. Besides the arguments over the bathroom, mid-compulsion confrontations and the dopey muscle-head friend, there were contamination fears having to do with the shared kitchen space. Jason, apparently, handled raw meats with something less than a religious adherence to FoodSafe guidelines. There was at least one instance, having to do with racial insensitivity, which Sanjay had brought up and then, seeming to regret having done so, just as quickly dismissed; when she had pressed him for details, he had kept things vague, and she hadn't felt it appropriate to squeeze any harder. Finally, and most frequently, there were the complaints about loud fighting and, even louder, reconciliatory sex between the roommate and his girlfriend. Jason's mercurial relationship with his lady had been enough of a passionate irritant that

Sanjay had invested in a pair of noise-cancelling headphones. After that, his mentions of the subject tapered off. What was Annick looking for? Why had she dived back in?

She realized, without noticing when it had started, that she was looking for it—looking for confirmation that he could, in fact, have done it. In the same way that her patients scanned for presence in order to confirm absence, Annick was looking for wells of rage. That way, when she didn't find any, she'd know that he was innocent.

At least that's what she told herself, shouting it internally to drown out another idea: maybe she did want to find some confirmation because that just wouldn't be as messy. And that wouldn't be her responsibility to fix.

And the fact was, she hadn't been there. Sanjay could have killed him.

Annick stood and chewed her bottom lip, and stared at the wall where her degree hung framed, with pride of place. Her years in Montréal had been her own chance for experimenting with copacetic and disagreeable roommates, stovetop-borne salmonella threats and sex-related noise violations, from the perspective of both offended and offending parties. Could she have killed any of them?

McGill was also where she had learned and honed her therapeutic philosophy and practice, her fanatical commitment to professional ethics and her exhaustive, encyclopedic knowledge of anxiety disorders. In nearly every conversation, she knew two or three times as much about her interlocutors as they made a point of telling her. With human beings both aware and oblivious of their position on the spectrum of anxiety behaviours, Annick brought a vast understanding of human failings and limitations, social obstacles and emotional motivations. She wondered, now, if she knew too much to see straight.

Dr. Annick Boudreau had studied this particular disorder in minute, all-encompassing detail; *Dr.* Annick Boudreau had spent about a dozen hours sharing a therapeutic presence with a young man named Sanjay Desai, but Annick Boudreau, human being, hadn't been in the apartment when Sanjay Desai's roommate had been killed. Before she threw herself into helping him, didn't she owe it to herself, to Sanjay, to the departed Jason MacGregor, to even contemplate the possibility that her patient had opened his throat? She caught her reflection in the corner of the glass framing her degree.

She stood nodding, looking herself in the eyes, as much because she didn't have any idea of where to start as anything else.

"No." She surprised herself by speaking out loud, surprised herself with her certainty. "Sanjay didn't do it. He did not kill that man. Now he's being held, in part, because of a clinical exercise that I asked him to engage in—and I was right to do it."

She rushed back over to the computer, and went back over her memories of her last appointment with Sanjay, and felt a surge of confidence as she remembered the story of the customer ejected from the nightclub—the East Side craft brewery and pizzeria owner who had been disciplined out of proportion to his social station, and who the bouncers had been worried might pose a problem.

Annick turned to her computer with electric excitement, opened her search engine and began combining search terms—"pizza," "craft brewery," "east side," "East Van," "chain"—until a profile began to emerge in the shape of Trevor Manning, a mid-thirties multimillionaire, in the mid-forties of the *Vancouver Magazine* "Power 50" rankings, smiling through brilliantly white teeth underneath the glow of a deep tan and the unmovable assurance of generational wealth.

Manning came from a major political family in the British Columbian interior, who over the course of 150 years had gone from leather-faced settlers to fruit and farming magnates to right-wing political dynasty; Trevor, unlike either his father or his grandfather, had never held provincial office, but there was still time. On page three of his search results was a news item about a fistfight in his late twenties, as well as an impaired driving arrest.

So here was a guy, almost certainly, from the sounds of it, an outright prick, with violence in his history and a grudge to nurse. Couldn't he have done the killing? Didn't it stand to reason?

Annick tried to think what an investigator might do beyond googling. She remembered a news story about an ICBC employee who sniffed out a several-hundred-thousand-dollar insurance fraud scheme using nothing but publicly visible social media posts. She checked the main sites, but Manning's Facebook account was private, and his Twitter had nothing but business tweets written in an anodyne, impersonal corporate style, alongside occasional postings from back home in peach country, which tended towards the conservative but stopped well short of customary online belligerence. Even then, there'd been nothing for almost a week.

The phone on her desk rang, and Annick recognized the number of Carl, a long-time patient with OCD, who had a tendency to phone looking for reassurance. Carl had a litany of ritual compulsions that were linked, in his mind, to the well-being and safety of family and friends. Like many patients with OCD, Carl ascribed to himself a kind of magical omnipotence, wherein it was within his power to keep everyone he knew safe from harm simply by performing his elaborate and time-consuming rituals—and the corollary of that power was that, if he didn't, and something were to happen, it would be his fault.

Carl knew that he shouldn't call Dr. Boudreau to seek reassurance, but he often felt as though he couldn't resist phoning anyway. They had a system: she would never pick up the first time. If he phoned again in thirty seconds, she would pick up and talk him down. These days he almost never did. And this time, he didn't either.

Annick laughed at herself, shaking her head, feeling suddenly cynical about her burst of detective enthusiasm. She had a skill set—several, in fact. But surely this wasn't it.

And moreover, what had made her feel like it was up to her? How different was her desire to prove her patient's innocence than Carl's quest to magically keep everyone who surrounded him healthy and safe?

She was Sanjay's therapist, and it was up to his lawyer to get him out of jail. After that, it would be up to her to walk him back from the trauma.

7

"ALLO, MA CHOUETTE."

"*Bonjour,* Maman."

Annick had fairly recently stopped FaceTiming or Skyping her mother on the other side of the country. For several years, the video chatting had been a balm for a family that had always been uncomplicatedly intimate and loving, were separated by vast geographical distance, but only geographical distance, and so could feel two or three times a week that they were all back in the same kitchen, that the salt water they all smelled came off of the same ocean. But recently, Annick had grown too irritated by, and claustrophobic from, the pileup of eulogies for her beautiful head of hair. It had happened too many times: her mother, Thérèse, creasing her facial features in heartbreak, asking if she'd really, really *had* to do it, offering empty repetitions of "*Je sais,* I know, *je sais*" when Annick had pointed out, flabbergasted, that Marie-Élaine, the little girl with leukemia for whom she'd shaved it in the first place, was her own granddaughter. In the time since, Annick had found that a return to the good, old-fashioned telephone call had liberated her from the judgment of the woman who had spent more than fifteen years brushing and braiding her daughter's cascading hair. It also gave Thérèse the plausible deniability to imagine that everything was still as it was when it came to her *bébé*'s head. If Annick's father, Roméo, had noticed any of it—the haircut or the switch from video to audio calls—he hadn't mentioned it.

Annick was calling now on the hands-free speaker in a miniature car-share vehicle she had picked up a few blocks from the clinic, and was now steering northward and eastward to make it to dinner with Supriya Desai. When she called from the cars, she never told her parents, because if she did, they would spend the rest of the conversation asking her if she was paying attention to the road.

"It's raining there?" asked Thérèse.

"No, the rain's *fini*... which is too bad, we could've used more of it. But it's a beautiful evening. You off to bed?"

"*Allo ma petite!*" cried Roméo over the speakerphone.

"*Allo* Papa."

"*T'es pas* in the car, *j'éspère*? Hunh?"

Annick smiled to herself as she took a left up Main Street, headed towards the mountains. "*Non.* Calling from the office."

"*Bon.* Talk to your mother."

"*C'est moi,*" Thérèse said, the increased clarity and volume indicating that she had picked up the receiver, and that it was now just the two girls.

"Where's he going?"

"*La toilette.*"

"Sorry I asked."

"He's spending so much time in there, Annick. Three, four times a day now, five. Not to pee, you know, but the other business. You're a doctor, you tell me—this is *normal*?"

"Luc is a doctor too, Maman, maybe you should ask him?"

"Hunh? Luc is a professor of history!"

"Exactly, and I'm a psychologist. The only time we talk about poop is in relation to anal retention. What does Dr. Breaux say?"

"I'm sorry, you have met Roméo Boudreau, or *non*? You think I can get him to go see Dr. Breaux? Maybe, he's on fire, I have a chance."

"I see," said Annick, passing under the viaducts and into Chinatown, turning off the air conditioning and rolling the windows down. The smells of Chinatown in the summertime, easier to pick up on foot but every now and then present for attentive motorists, were a Proustian reminder of the trip that she and Philip had taken to Hong Kong three summers earlier, for her to meet his grandparents. The medicinal, oceanic smells of dried goods displayed in large, open containers always took her back, and simultaneously reminded her of the more charming Vancouver of the time of her arrival, a stark contrast to today's glittering, botoxed version of the city.

Annick sighed. "Is he showing any other symptoms?"

"See? Like I say, you're a doctor."

"Maman! I'm asking what any teenager knows to type into WebMD."

"I don't know it."

"Don't worry about it. Does he have any other symptoms?"

"He's very low energy, *toujours fatigué*. I have to wake him up, these days."

Annick frowned. This was, indeed, very peculiar behaviour with regard to Roméo Boudreau. Raised by a fisherman, her grandfather Dieudonné, Roméo had spent his entire life waking in anticipation of the sun; Annick had never known her father to open his eyes onto daylight—he always beat it. Roméo made the coffee, began preparing breakfast, woke his wife; none of the Boudreau kids had ever seen him unshaven on a weekday, aside from the brushy moustache that was still, at age sixty-seven, the same reddish brown it had always been, despite his head of fully silver hair.

"Fuck yourself, cocksucker!" screamed a shirtless man with arms covered in scabs, engaging an invisible enemy on the opposite sidewalk. Annick cringed.

"Annick! Are you in the car?"

"*Non, non,* Maman," she promised as she rolled up the windows, slipped the air conditioning back on and prepared to turn off Main and onto Hastings. "Is there anything else besides his being tired?"

"Well, the *toilette.*"

"No, I know. I mean besides that."

Annick could hear her mother in the grips of an uncharacteristic hesitation. When she spoke again, it was in a whisper.

"No, in the toilet. He—oh, he will be angry."

"Maman, what?"

"We had a problem here, last weekend. The toilet plugged. I flush it and the last *mouvement,* it came back up."

"Okay. For the record, this is very gross."

"But Annick, it was all red. *Rouge, rouge, rouge.*"

"Jesus Christ—like in *The Conversation*?"

"What conversation, you think I can get him to talk about it?"

"No, Maman, it's a Gene Hackman movie."

"No, I'm telling you, it happened!"

"No, I know. I—just give me a second, okay? I need to pull over."

"Annick! You promise!"

"I never promised anything."

Annick pulled over to the curb, parking in front of an architecturally anomalous yellow building, done in a Spanish style in stark contrast to the functional, mid-century-invisible buildings surrounding it. She had always wondered about the building, without ever having been curious enough to look into what it was. At present, she didn't even notice it.

"Maman, I don't have to be a medical doctor to tell you that those are—that's a very troubling combination of symptoms. Papa has to see Dr. Breaux."

"He's worked so hard, *toute sa vie*."

"I know."

"I light the candle every Sunday..."

"Yes, Maman, and that's good—but he also needs to see Dr. Breaux."

"*Je ne sais pas.*"

Annick slapped her hand on the dashboard, eliciting a short, sharp gasp from her mother. She ran her hand over her face, extricating herself for a moment from the problems of the world, from a patient in jail for a murder he didn't commit on one side of the country, and a father with blood in his stools on the other. Two men separated by six provinces, by language, by skin colour, by social class and by about forty years, but neither of them willing, or able, to level with their families about the state of their health. She swallowed the two seconds of ungenerosity that made her want to leave them to their own stubborn, cowardly devices.

She closed her eyes. "Maman, I have to go to dinner now, to a meeting."

"Is everything okay?"

"I have a patient who is going through a very great difficulty at the moment."

"He is so lucky to have you."

It was all Annick could do to hold back a laugh, despite everything, at her mother's hairpin shift in tone. Thérèse Leblanc was a largely unsentimental woman who nevertheless loved her family above all other things—if that love expressed itself in worry about a serious threat to her husband's health, it could shoot up just as suddenly in a volcanic expression of pride over her daughter, the talented and devoted psychologist, soothing troubled minds on the shores of the Pacific.

"Maman, talk to Papa. Tell him I said he has to go see Dr. Breaux, and that every day he waits before making an appointment, I bring in another sibling or cousin on the campaign to get him there."

Thérèse tsked, despite herself. "Annick."

"I'll call you tomorrow, okay?"

"*Je t'aime fort, ma petite chouette.*"

"*Je t'aime,* Maman."

8

ARWA NABULSI COULD not legally travel to the city of her birth, and now she lived, and cooked, and ran a restaurant on land that had never been legally handed over to the people who currently governed it. When Annick had recounted to her the history of her own ancestors, a gaggle of French-speaking Catholics expelled on pain of death from a country that they snuck back into over the next several centuries, Arwa had smiled bleakly, shaken her head and brought out a plate of chicken that Annick hadn't ordered. Arwa's husband, Mahmoud, a conceptual artist, had abandoned a celebrated practice as a sculptor, explaining—in an eleven-thousand-word blog post that went viral without anyone's having read it all the way to the end—that in a world marked by the struggle for territory, his art would no longer take up anything but a superficial physical space. Mahmoud now worked exclusively in two dimensions, which, he would always point out, was still one dimension more than Arabs ever got to inhabit in film and television. A new series of photographs, *Refugee/ Settler*—black and white photos of a checkered Palestinian keffiyeh flying from the masts of sailboats, from ski-slope chairlifts, even serving as a beachside picnic blanket—was now being mounted on the walls of the Jerusalem Artichoke by an eager pair of proteges under Mahmoud's manic, artistically authoritarian eyes.

"While you wait," Arwa said, setting a small glass of thick, black Turkish coffee down in front of Annick, the smell of cardamom like a soft hand running down her arm.

"Oh, Arwa," Annick said ecstatically. "*Que tu es merveilleuse.*"

"*Je vous en prie,*" smiled Arwa, and the Middle Eastern–inflected French, coupled with the smell of the coffee, reminded Annick of a summer she'd spent in Montréal with a Tunisian man named Isa, in which they had passed what felt like weeks without ever standing vertically. A few years later, Isa had been elected to Québec's National Assembly as a member of the sovereigntist party. But if his political focus was now narrowly on Québec, Annick would never forget the effectiveness and gentleness of his previous outreach to the Acadian community.

"Lady," said Mahmoud, snapping her out of her reverie, "I don't know where you just went, but I think we'd all like to go there." She swatted him gently with her menu.

A woman with a perfect face twisted into an impossible agony of fear and despair came in through the front door of the restaurant, and Annick knew immediately that it was Supriya. She stood instinctively, placing a coffee cup emptied of all but the acrid silt at the bottom back onto its glass saucer. Supriya looked like royalty in mourning—endowed with an elegance that wouldn't camouflage under duress, but which was politely demurring under a simple ponytail and absence of cosmetics, stale wrinkled clothing and rolled-up sleeves.

"Dr. Boudreau?" she said, in a posh-sounding British accent, and Annick nodded, trying to read Supriya's inscrutable body language, wondering whether to offer a handshake, a hand to the elbow, a hug? Instead, they stood woodenly in each other's presence for a moment, before nodding and sitting down.

"Do you feel like you could eat, Dr. Desai?"

"Supriya, please."

"Sure, and Annick."

"Thank you, Annick. I'm not entirely certain—I have a feeling of both overwhelming hunger along with an almost total aversion."

"Why don't I order us something and we can both pick at it, together?"

"Yes, thank you. Annick, while you order, I'm going to excuse myself to splash some water on my face?"

"Of course."

Supriya stood and strode to the washrooms at the back of the restaurant, and Annick waved Arwa down and put in an order for lamb over rice and *mutabal*, the smoky eggplant dish served with triangles of whole wheat pita just slightly thicker than Mahmoud's recent artistic output. When Supriya sat back down at the table, Annick noticed that the splash of water had rejuvenated her face to an extent that would take most people a week in the sun of Mediterranean France.

"How is Sanjay? I mean, given the circumstances?"

Supriya closed her eyes, raised one shoulder and shook her head for longer than a lesser person could have gotten away with. "He's absolutely lost. It's a mother's nightmare, I promise you. This poor boy—he has always been my poor boy." Several large tears ran surreptitiously down Supriya's cheeks, down tracks that had already been used many times that day. Annick reached a hand out across the table, and Supriya took it up greedily, stroking it without embarrassment or reservation. "It is such a difficult thing to raise a gentle boy. Sometimes I feel like there is no axis that this world turns on that wasn't set to grind him down." Annick noticed now that there were Indian notes in behind the upper-class British music of her voice, and somehow they conspired to make even the most grandiloquent sentences seem perfectly normal. Supriya wiped her hands across her cheeks, clattering together several lacquered wooden bracelets. "He has this way of looking, setting his eyes—one moment he seems to be begging me to save him, to pull him out from there, while at the next he looks almost like he believes he deserves it."

"Being in jail?"

"Steve Biko said that the most powerful weapon in the hands of the oppressor is the mind of the oppressed. When a young man has been criminalized, he can actually begin to believe that he's guilty."

"Did he say that?"

"No, no, not in words—of course not. But he has this tragic *guilt* in his countenance. I can't bear it. Some sort of shame he won't articulate to me."

Annick nodded her head. "Supriya, you understand of course that my sessions with Sanjay are entirely confidential, and that without his explicit permission, I can't share anything of our work together with you?"

"Yes, I'm aware. Of course, of course. I understand."

"Has he mentioned anything to his lawyer about me? Does his lawyer want to bring me in?"

Supriya nodded again, her face gone for a moment in an absent contemplation, then sharpening back into focus. "He'd like to hold off."

"He'd like the Crown to bring me in instead?"

"That's the sense that I got, yes. Do you know anything about this so-called murder journal?"

Arwa arrived with the *mutabal* just in time to save Annick from having to deliver another, more detailed lecture on confidentiality. The two women sat in silence for a minute, first staring at the plate, then picking at it tentatively, before they each realized how much hungrier they were than they'd first thought. Nothing was said as they scooped the eggplant, with its sheen of olive oil, into their grateful mouths. Before the conversation had had a chance to resume, Arwa brought their perfect lamb, meat piled high on a bed of tartly pickled cabbage and soft white rice, staining with the juices of the meat. They avoided discussing the fate of their patient and son for a few minutes longer, rectifying the negligence that each of them had paid their bodies over the course of the day. Finally, Annick spoke.

"Do you have a sense of the case being made against him?"

"They say that they have him unambiguously," Supriya answered with an ironic incredulity. "Sanjay could have gone to Simon Fraser University for free, of course, because of my being a faculty member there, but he's too stubbornly independent for that, as you can well imagine. So instead he's off to UBC, and rather than living in our home, in Burnaby, he insists he wants to live in this awful basement suite in Kitsilano that he found on the internet, helping some horrible petty bourgeois couple pay for their kitchen renovations by renting a room next to a fascist thug." Supriya waited for Annick to agree with her that this was crazy, but when she didn't, it didn't seem to matter much. "It's all crazy, of course. These same upstairs landlords heard yelling on the night the roommate died. They phoned the police, who arrived to find Sanjay in the bathroom, they say scrubbing his hands and forearms meticulously, listening to music as though nothing of any great occasion had transpired."

Annick noticed that the once-"odious" Jason had now graduated into full-fledged fascism, but decided not to say anything just yet.

"Sanjay was listening to music?"

"Yes—and of course Sanjay explained to them that this was precisely why he was unaware that anything had happened, you see? He has a pair of noise-cancelling headphones that I bought for him, and through them, if he has music playing, he can't hear anything at all."

"Is that all they have on him? That he was there, washing his hands?"

"That and the journal, and the landlords saying they'd heard fighting before. When they found the other blood, they tried to tell him that it would be easier for him if he turned over his so-called accomplice—"

"Wait, the other blood?"

"Yes, they found blood at the scene that appears to be neither Jason's nor Sanjay's. They are using this third person both to threaten my son and to tempt him into a plea deal. To induce him, they say his cooperation will lead to greater leniency—to terrify him, they say that they'll find the other victim, who is in hiding."

"But the idea," Annick said, feeling both vindicated in her instincts about Sanjay's innocence and guilty for having doubted it at all, "that this mystery blood could be the murderer's isn't even being considered?"

"Why would it? The way it is, they have the whole thing off their ledgers, with a community activist silenced from shame in the process. Or so they think. But I think they'll find I won't go quietly. If they believe I'll stand by while my son's life is negated because the world lost this vicious non-entity..."

"You mean Jason MacGregor?"

Supriya's tongue angrily searched the front of her closed mouth, her face furrowing severely. Without looking at Annick, she reached jumpily for her glass of water and, instead, knocked it over.

"Oh, Jesus," she said, shooting back from the table and standing.

"It's okay," said Annick, in her most clinically reassuring voice, standing to wipe the puddle with her napkin, and a handful more brought over by Arwa. When Supriya's glass had been refilled, she took a long draw from it, closed her eyes and took several deep breaths in through her nose.

"I cannot begin to imagine how hard this is for you, Supriya."

"Thank you, Doctor," Supriya said, her eyes reopening but still not meeting Annick's. "Jason MacGregor was a predictable excrescence of this country's toxic hierarchies and codes of exclusion. Sanjay has always been, to my chagrin, somewhat timid in the face of these sorts of provocations. I don't have the same hesitations, as I'm sure you've come to guess by now. He once called Sanjay 'Osama,' which was not only hateful but entirely incoherent. He told Sanjay just after he'd moved in that he didn't want the kitchen to end up smelling 'like an Indian restaurant.'"

"This guy just gets more and more charming."

"I told Sanjay that if he wasn't willing to say anything, that I would say something in his place."

"Oh. And how did Sanjay respond to that?"

"Much like you did just now, Doctor."

Annick smiled. "Annick, please. And sorry, if I winced, it had more to do with the... the *complexities* of the parent-child relationship, and not any political disagreements. It sounds like the roommate was a bigoted twerp."

"The personal *is* political, of course, Annick. Nevertheless, I understand your point. And the few times that I met Jason, I managed to hold myself back, though I was physically seething."

"Sure."

"You have no idea what it's like to send a vulnerable child out into the world and then feel like you cannot protect him."

Annick tried to sort through the details that Supriya had offered. She absentmindedly picked at the stray, gravy-soaked grains of rice at the fringes of the plate. Wherever her mind was taking her, the ringing of Supriya's phone ripped her back from it.

"Yes, hello?"

Annick watched Supriya's face.

"No. No, no, no—that's impossible. Oh, I won't stand for this, we won't stand for this. His safety is your responsibility! No, no. Yes? No, that's—oh, please! No, I'll be right back there. You are—I'm holding you all absolutely responsible for this!" Supriya hung up her phone and threw it into her large, woven silk bag, standing. "Sanjay has been beaten by a group of other prisoners."

Annick leapt to her feet. "Oh, Supriya! Go to him, I'll take care of this. Let him know that I'm here, whatever you two need. And tell his lawyer that I'm ready whenever it's best."

"Yes," Supriya said, turning to leave. "Yes, alright. Thank you."

"Supriya?"

"Yes?"

"Tell Sanjay that he hasn't done anything wrong. And that he should be as honest with you as he can be."

For the first time, Supriya's face turned to anger.

"And what is that supposed to mean? What are you suggesting, Doctor?"

"Sanjay will know what I mean, Supriya. Please trust me."

"Trust," Supriya said with an acid smile, as though the very concept were an affront. "I have to take care of my son."

Supriya moved through the restaurant at the fastest pace possible without running, turned towards her car parked somewhere along Hastings, and was gone. Arwa had made her way over to the table, and she reached a hand out to Annick's elbow.

"Is everything okay, Annick?"

"No," Annick said, shaking her head. "No. Things are really, really bad."

~

Rather than booking another car share, Annick decided to take one of the creaking electric cable buses running westbound along Hastings Street, through the sedimentary layers of Vancouver's history of class war, falling fortunes and renewed leases on life: along the thoroughfare were blocks of the city as it had once been, bruised and bruising, worse for wear, and there were glossed and polished blocks that had largely shed the gravity of the city's social past, with specialty cheese shops and Italian scooter dealerships, and in between there were aspirational blocks, in transition between the two, with well-guarded convenience stores abutting condo marketing storefronts and juice companies. Along the north side of the street, across from the Finnish steam baths that had been there since 1926—and whose private saunas had been the site of Annick and Philip's fourth date, and venue for their first physical intimacies (and second and third, depending on how you counted)—Annick caught sight of a thin, stylish neon peach sign spelling, in cursive, "The O.K. Pizza &

Ravioli Company: Est. 2017." Before even realizing what she was doing, Annick pulled the bell.

As the engine noise of the cable-powered bus slowly died, the driver lurching the vehicle towards the bus stop at a slant, Annick felt a pounding in her ears that she tried to ignore. It was true—this wasn't her business. She had no authority to ask Trevor Manning any questions, nor even any particular reasons to think that he'd done it, despite the recent altercation at the club where Jason and his best friend bounced. Without particularly understanding why, though, she felt like she owed it to Sanjay.

Inside, O.K. Pizza looked like almost every other restaurant in any other part of the world, with found elements from a real or imagined industrial past burnished to decorative beauty. A long-beam counter separated the dining area from an enormous, wood-burning pizza oven done in colourful mosaic, set apart from three large, silver tanks for brewing beer by an open-concept kitchen in the middle. TV screens bore the whimsical, locally inspired names of various craft brews—Ross Street IPA; East Van Cross Pilsner; Michael J. Hops Witbier—as well as ever-dwindling percentage numbers indicating how much of each beer was left.

Annick was approached by an enthusiastic and forgettably beautiful young man with red cheeks and a table towel in his hand.

"Hi! This your first time here?"

"It is, yeah," said Annick, smiling winningly. "The pizza's just okay?"

"Naw, we get that all the time. The O.K. stands for Okanagan."

"Ah, gotcha."

"The boss is a Kelowna boy."

"That's Trevor, right?"

"Yeah! You know Trevor?"

"Actually, I was hoping that maybe I could speak to him?"

The waiter had a face that didn't much register confusion, because a kind of blank, open, questioning look was its default. He pushed through, his smile faltering only briefly.

"Are you looking for a job?"

"Um," said Annick, not sure how she planned to approach asking Manning about his altercation with Jason MacGregor, not sure how she would assess whether or not he was capable of murder. "Yeah."

"Hold on one second," said the young man, confidently in the saddle again and heading off towards another corner of the large dining area.

She would scrutinize Manning's physical bearing, his demeanour—any suggestion of seething roughness, of potential violence, even a seething anger, like Supriya's. She'd try to scan for any signs of the fallout from a fight, black eyes or scraped hands. When she'd exhausted all of that, she would float Jason MacGregor's name, mention the nightclub, anything that might twig an incriminating response.

"You were expecting someone else?"

Annick must have let her face show the full range of her surprise when a thin, stern-faced middle-aged man of medium height and conventionally gay presentation put his hand out for a cold and cursory shake.

"Oh, no, sorry, I just—I thought he was going to get Trevor."

Clinically, without any lust or desire, the man took Annick in head to toe, with a special emphasis on chest to knees, and somehow it felt even more objectifying than if he had seemed to enjoy it.

PRIMARY OBSESSIONS

"How long have you been waitressing?"

"Me? I don't really—I mean, it's..."

Her interviewer stretched his eyebrows up impatiently, jutting out his chin.

"Well?"

"I was actually—is Trevor here?"

"No."

"Oh. Is, um—do you know if he's coming back soon?"

At this, the manager crossed his arms across his thin chest, his face tightening in a mask of skeptical contempt.

"And sorry, why would I provide private information about the whereabouts of our employees to someone just in off the street?"

"Well, he's not your employee, he's your boss," Annick said, finding her footing now, lofted by the rudeness of her interlocutor into an adrenaline sharpness. "And we grew up together in Kelowna and I was hoping to surprise him. Sorry, can I please have your name?"

The man's countenance dissolved instantly and reconfigured entirely in obsequious and conspiratorial friendliness. "Oh, I am so sorry—Aiden said you were looking for a job! Meanwhile, I'm thinking, 'If she can afford a suit this nice, what's she need this job for?' Right?"

Annick smiled perfunctorily. "Is he here?"

"Oh no, sweetie—Trevor's still on the Amalfi."

"The Amalfi Coast?"

Her eager new friend nodded. "Left a week ago, not back for another two."

"*Shit.*"

"Aw, I know. I'd be happy to tell him you came by? What was your name again?"

"Sam," said Annick, smiling through her frustration at losing the suspect who was never really a suspect, angry at

70

herself again for playing private investigator when she had no business butting in and no idea of what it was she was doing. "Sam Spade."

9

THERE WAS SOMETHING about a pour-over coffee that felt perversely ecstatic for Annick—an ecumenical mix of the dark, sensual caffeination of Catholic café societies with the deferred gratification of the Protestant ethic. The three minutes during which Annick hung her crewcut over the counter at Calibre Coffee—bleary-eyed and aching with want as a barista still committed to a woolly toque–wearing aesthetic in the midst of summer poured scalding water through the magic beans—were the longest three minutes of her day. The longest, but in some ways the most fulfilling. Here were a body and a mind screaming to her that they couldn't last another second without coffee, and here she was forcing them to.

Today there was the added wait of the walk to the seats out front, because lo, the heavens had parted: Dr. Annick Boudreau had the morning off, and she was ordering her coffee to stay. She slipped her big tortoiseshell sunglasses over her eyes, triumphantly returned a flirtatious smile from a woman who couldn't have been more than twenty-two and sat down on a wooden bench just off the eastern wall of the red and yellow Dominion Building, a historic piece of ketchup-and-mustard Edwardian architecture that had once been the tallest building in the British Empire, and whose overhang now kept pot-smokers dry on rainy days.

Annick nearly checked her phone before taking her first sip, then decided that she had delayed gratification for long enough already, and that she had suffered sufficiently in order to enjoy her due. Every one of the tasting notes that, on her more cynical days, she assumed they must be pulling out of the air, today stood up on her tongue and proudly declared its presence: tones of hazelnuts and persimmon, dark chocolate and post-war compromise; lavender, citrus and Mom and Dad getting back together. She must have been showing the full extent of her shuddering enjoyment of those first few sips, because when she looked back at the twenty-two year old, she was blushing.

Over the years, Annick had had to train herself to allow for moments of complete liberation from the suffering of others, so that she could more effectively attend to it in the other hours of the day. It was a lesson she had learned years ago from her practicum supervisor, Dr. Philomena Conte, a woman who'd been at it so long she'd practically been able to tell Jung he was too soft on the Nazis in real time. Dr. Conte had held on fiercely to the non-sentimentality of her weather-beaten Calabrian grandparents, trying to replicate the steady hand with which they had slaughtered beloved pigs in the course of her own more emotionally sensitive labours. Annick had reported to her supervisor that she'd found herself crying, hours after a session with a young woman whose equally young husband had died. Dr. Conte had been less than indulgent in her reply.

"You try to carry the ocean with you, all you're gonna do is drown," Philomena had told her, and Annick had never had the courage to ask if that was a certified, heirloom aphorism or just a diamond that she had squeezed by force out of the coal of psychological practice. Regardless, the lesson had stuck. Some of the time.

Halfway through her cup, though, Annick allowed herself to think it all through one more time. If someone who was neither Sanjay nor Jason nor the avenging millionaire Trevor Manning had bled in the room, that person was almost certainly the one who'd opened Jason's throat. Supriya hadn't mentioned anything about them having found a murder weapon, and clearly that would be in Sanjay's favour. It would have been someone that Jason would have let into the house, someone he knew. Someone he would have struggled with, been able to briefly overpower, or at least wound badly. She smiled ruefully, feeling idiotic. Of course.

Manning had seemed such an obvious candidate that Annick had entirely overlooked Jason's girlfriend, his partner in their mutually destructive *amour fou*. Given the dramatic cleavages between the couple, the thunderstorm clashes and recouplings that Sanjay had recounted, didn't it stand to reason that the girl might finally have snapped off from the tether that had provided all that magical tension? Statistically, it was much more likely to have started in the other direction, and that was still possible: say the girl came over, they went to the bedroom for some grab-ass, and along the way, it melted into one of their operatic confrontations. This time, though, it turned physical. Maybe he had attacked her with the knife, stopped in his tracks when he saw the blood, dropped the knife and begged forgiveness just long enough for her to stick him in the neck.

That may not have been exactly how it had happened, but if Annick could come up with it, surely the girl's lawyer could spin something similarly convincing. The poor thing was probably hiding, terrified, but once Sanjay explained his ocd and allowed his lawyer to call Annick in to clarify the thought journal, they would find her and the truth would get out—or a version of it that might even allow the girlfriend

74

to claim that she had acted in self-defence. The more she played it over in her mind, the more sense it made.

At the end of the thought, Annick heard a surreal ping, as though she'd guessed something correctly in a cartoon; it was a full two seconds before she realized that it had been an incoming email on her phone.

The message had the subject line COMMENT? and it came from Ryan Devlin, the CBC producer who had arranged the panel with the screenwriter. Reading the body of the email, Annick had the same instant, painful nausea she'd experienced the time the handle end of a hockey stick had speared her stomach in the corner of the elementary school gym.

Hi Dr. Boudreau—

Wondering if you are available to speak on a panel this afternoon, preceded by a radio one-on-one if we could, about the whole Sanjay Desai mental health thing?
Please give me a ring,

Ryan

Just exactly what *fucking* Sanjay Desai mental health *thing* was he talking about? Annick was across Hastings Street in seconds, shooting past the World War I memorial at Victory Square before she even realized that she was running to the CBC building. She hadn't even told Cedric, hadn't even told Philip, that Sanjay Desai was her patient. How in sweet hell was it possible that a journalist from the public broadcasting corporation was now asking her to speak on TV and radio about his mental health? As she sped up Cambie Street, past the Queen Elizabeth Theatre and into the shadow of the Roman Colosseum–shaped library building, Annick could see Dr. Conte shaking her head derisively.

"*You're losing it, kid.*"

Barely able to speak as she struggled for breath, Annick asked the security guard first in French, then in English, then in French again, to call Ryan to the front lobby, regardless of what he was doing. A few minutes later, after she'd very nearly caught up to all of her breathing, her heart rate now slightly below that of a hummingbird, Ryan waltzed into the front lobby with a look of relaxation and calm on his face that was almost offensive.

"Hey, look at this—panellist is here in thirty minutes or it's free..."

"Ryan, what the hell was that email about?"

In an instant, Ryan's face was no longer offensive.

"What do you mean?"

"What do you mean what do I mean? How does my name come up in conjunction with Sanjay Desai?"

"I mean, no particular reason, except that you're our mental health gal," Ryan answered, then realized he'd said "gal." "Expert. You're—you always, you're the first call we make when we need an expert to come in and talk about mental health, or mental health stigma. And this other guy's Facebook post, the victim's friend? It's already gone viral. It's insane."

Annick winced as hard as she could, but no second coffee materialized in her hands—she would have to cut through her obliterating confusion by other means.

"Ryan, I don't know what you are talking about. What friend? What Facebook post?"

"You telling me you haven't checked the news this morning?"

"I had the morning off. It'll be my last one until I retire, I promise. Just start at the beginning and pretend I'm coming out of a coma."

"The kid they arrested the other day, he killed his room-mate—allegedly killed his roommate. The kid's name is Sanjay Desai, mid-twenties, student out at UBC. They're holding him because they figure it's open and shut. He'd written down violent fantasies in a diary, and he was washing off when the cops got there."

Relief flooded into every corner of Annick's body. Ryan seemed to have no idea that he was her patient.

"But the kid who got killed, he worked at a club, down-town, Babylon Rivers? Basically it's like a part nightclub, part strip club and, unofficially, it sounds like basically a brothel maybe, anyway sex parties and all of it."

"Okay. I feel like maybe we're getting off course here..."

"Hey, not fair. You said coma."

Annick gave a concessionary nod.

"Anyway, the kid who got killed was a doorman at this club, and one of the other bouncers, his buddy, has posted this absolutely venomous, like, *screed* on Facebook about how our society coddles people with mental illness, refuses to protect normal people—the thing's been liked by twenty thousand people, re-shared like five thousand times."

"Oh, Jesus."

Ryan fished his cellphone out of the front pocket of his tan jeans. "Here," he said, offering it to Annick. She took it in her hands, and read. The status was next to a profile photo of a man named Mike Collis, who looked big even in a thumb-nail image, wearing dark sunglasses and holding a large fish.

I HAVE HAD IT POLITICAL CORRECTNESS CAN ABSOLUTELY GO FUCK IT SELF BECAUSE I JUST

LOST THE BEST BUDDY I EVER HAD IN MY LIFE TO A ***VIOLENT*** *****MENTALLY ILL SCUMBAG MURDERER. O SORRY I FORGOT ON THE NEWS YOUR SUPPOSED TO SAY "ALLEGEDLY" BUT FUCK THAT ILL SAY HIS NAME****** SANJAY DESAI MURDERED MY BEST FRIEND JASON MACGREGOR RIP. SLIT HIS THROAT OPEN LIKE GODAMED LAMM TO THE SLOGHTER. I DONT CARE IF SOME GUYS SAY CRYING IS FAGOT FUCK THAT I CRIED MY EYES OUT ALL DAMM NIGHT. IF THERES ONE THING WORSE THAN LOOSING A FRIEND TO DEATH OR SHOULD I SAY *********MURDER****** ITS KNOWING THAT THEY COULD OF STOPPED IT BEFORE IT EVER HAPPENED. YA THATS RIGHT SANJAY ""SCUMBAG""DESAI IS FUCKED IN THE HEAD AND JASON KNEW IT AND TOLD IT TO HIS LANDLORD THIS GUY IS MENTALLY ILL OFFICIALLY. SORRY I GUESS THATS THE POLITICALLY CORRECT WAY OF SAYING NUT JOB BUT EVEN THO JASON WAS SCARED OF THIS PYSCO THE LANDLORD SAID HIS HUMAN RIGHTS WERE IN VIOLLATION IF THEY KICKED HIM OUT. SORRY THIS IS WHERE POLITICAL CORRECTNESS LANDED US TOO WHERE MENTALLY ILLS HAVE MORE RIGHTS THAN A NORMAL PERSON AND WE ARE AT THERE DISPOSURE PLANE AND SIMPLE. WHEN ARE THE REST OF US GONNA JUST SAY ENOUGH I HOPE THAT DAY WILL SOON TO COME BUT ITS ALREADY TOO LATE FOR MY BEST FRIEND. *********RIP***** MY BROTHER JASON WILL NEVER FORGET YOU OR THE LIFE YOU LEAD. YOUR LOVED IN ARE HEARTS AND MAYBE CANADA WILL FINALLY GET THE WAKE UP CALL

THAT ITS NOT MENTAL ILLNESS ITS JUST PLANE
CRAZY AND THE REST OF US HAVE RIGHTS TO
AND THATS DEFENDING OURSELVES I MISS YOU
BROTHER

Annick stared at the phone for a few seconds after she'd
read the status a third time. Without looking up, she handed
it back to Ryan.

"So... can you do the panel?"

Ryan regretted the question the moment Annick met his
gaze, everything perfectly still and calm except for the wall
of rage covering each of her eyes like cataracts.

"No."

"I understand."

"No, Cedric is doing the media for the clinic for the next
little bit."

"Dr. Manley? The mindfulness guy?"

"Yeah. Phone him, he'll come down."

"Cool, thanks Annick. You gonna be okay?"

"I'm already okay, Ryan. Thanks. If you see Philip at his
desk, can you please send him out to the JJ Bean in front?"

"Absolutely."

"I'm going to get another coffee."

10

"NOW, I HOPE that my asking this doesn't come across as overly sensitive, but—is there something wrong with our sex life?"

Annick turned to Philip and smiled, trying to be playful with his confusion when really she hadn't thought through how she would explain any of this to him at all, why they were here, in a strip club, or what she was looking for. She hadn't thought through an explanation for Philip not only because of the questions of confidentiality at play, but also because an explanation would have presumed that she knew what she was doing herself.

"And what if I told you that asking that did, in fact, make you sound overly sensitive?"

"I guess, in that case, I would still be curious as to what we were doing in a frat-boy flesh club, with you wearing a pair of booty shorts that leave less to the imagination than an MRI," said Philip, looking down into his glass. "Then I'd probably order another seven-dollar mug of ginger ale– flavoured ice cubes."

Annick smiled apologetically at Philip, who had every right to have a chip on his shoulder; there was no room on either of Annick's, because her earrings were too big.

"I told you, we're undercover."

"Apparently, yeah. Cover so deep even your partner doesn't know what we're doing."

Annick supposed she should be grateful to have a boyfriend bored, rather than titillated, by the Babylon Rivers nightclub. If the Roman Empire had managed to survive into the twenty-first century, and one of the Caesars had raised a middle son particularly lacking in imagination, this was the pleasure palace that son would have commissioned. Downstairs, a throbbing and more or less run-of-the-mill dance club pounded indistinguishable tracks through speakers that vibrated throughout the main room, next to television screens running soft-core pornography; the men's washrooms had advertisements on the wall for sports cars and condominiums, and the women's washrooms had public service announcements reminding patrons not to leave open drinks out of their sight.

Up a steep flight of stairs which seemed designed in anticipation of short skirts, patrons with slightly deeper pockets or slightly more insistent erections could sit, as Annick and Philip were now, at raised tables bordering a hard, clear plastic stage emanating a shade of pink-purple light not to be found in nature, featuring a show centred around breasts that couldn't be found in nature either. Waitresses in denim shorts cut to nearly gynecological lengths brought drinks with prices listed in the inflated numbers of Weimar Germany, and massage girls could also be hired to listlessly rub the necks and shoulders of audience members feeling particularly imperial, or having just inherited the family's car dealership after their father's massive coronary or ahi tuna–related mercury poisoning.

The lithe and superhumanly patient women onstage scaled and descended three different poles with such stunning athleticism that Philip's anti-erotic ennui was briefly edged out by the enthusiasm of his science journalist's instincts: "Do you realize the kind of leg strength a move like that requires?"

Behind the stage, past the bar, a small but steady procession of more substantial and decidedly more terrifying men intermittently made their way towards a doorway which implied yet a third Dantean circle of adolescent sexual fantasy made manifest, for customers rolling even higher than those copping back rubs at stage left. Sipping her own drink of vodka and 7UP, charmingly listed as Panty Peeler on the cocktail menu, Annick had noticed a large man guarding the doorway to the next level of debauchery. He wore a black dress shirt with every button done up, hanging untucked over a pair of shiny pants, and he had been accepting well-wishing handshakes, shoulder slaps and sundry other masculine enactments of congratulation the whole time they'd been here. It was Mike Collis.

Annick stood, pulling her red cotton shorts with white piping up to her ribs, then rolling the waistband down low enough to show her belly button. Philip stared at her in confusion.

"You still worried about our sex life?" she asked playfully, collecting her drink from the table.

"Annick," said Philip seriously. "What is going on? I'm not remotely enjoying this. Why are we here? It isn't funny anymore."

Annick tried and failed to keep the fun, flirtatious look on her face, wincing through the broken pieces of a smile.

"I'm sorry, Philip. I just have to check something. It'll be five more minutes, tops. Please trust me when I say it's not something that I can outline in all its details to you, but that everything is going to be okay."

Philip shook his head wistfully, then turned back to the stage.

"Okay, I guess. Do what you gotta do." Then, jerking his thumb towards the dancers, he added: "Just hurry up before I fall in love with another."

Involuntarily, Annick found herself moving with the music that scored the performances, walking towards the back of the room with a heavy, hip-driven gait that wasn't really hers. She practised smiling with her tongue pressed against her top teeth, dipping her chin girlishly. As she approached Mike Collis, she briefly hid her face in a sip of Panty Peeler.

There were men who could hide when they were assessing a woman physically, and there were men who couldn't—but there was a third group of men for whom hiding the act of assessment went against the very purpose of sizing a woman up in the first place. Such men, like Mike Collis, splashed their gaze the way the lower-order mammals did urine, in a show of control, supremacy, sovereignty. Mike took her in from head to toe as though he were an airport security officer and she were a perfectly innocent computer engineer born in Pakistan: entirely, and mercilessly. He even craned the space between his head and his shoulders that should have been a neck in order to show that he was taking in what he could of her backside from where he stood. Against every impulse screaming in every cell of her recently scanned body, Annick gratefully took his attention as though it were a paper cup of water passed to a marathon runner by a good Samaritan.

"What do you have to do to get back there?" she asked him playfully, doing her best to stay seductive at the decibel level necessary in the throbbing club.

"Talent like you? I could get you back there no problem."

"You're sweet."

"If I had you sitting on my face, I wouldn't hear Mom calling me for dinner."

Annick came dangerously close to laughing, and caught herself by biting her lip, hard, which worked out well because Mike read it as flirtation.

"What's with that hair, though? You in the army or something?"

"Oh, are you negging me now? Are we already at the negging part?" Annick silently cursed herself for not being able to control her sarcasm. If this dumb gorilla was working decade-and-a-half-old pickup techniques, it didn't matter to her—it's not like she was going to fall for them. But the implication that she was smarter than him was likely to shut things down quickly, and with prejudice. She could already see the anger on his face.

"I don't give a fuck, bitch."

"No, no—I liked what you said."

"What, about your hair?"

"No, about where I could sit," she said, smiling into her drink, the ice cubes clinking down onto her upper lip, as Mike tried to hide a shit-eating smile. "I like that you don't give a fuck about what's politically correct."

Mike's face became instantly more serious, and he straightened his posture.

"Yeah? I just speak my mind how it is," he said. "I guess you saw my post."

Annick took another sip of the vodka and 7UP, this time for courage.

"I knew Jason," she said, hesitating slightly as she waited for him to explode with rage; when he didn't immediately reject her claim, she pressed on with it. "When he was a kid. He went to school with my little brother." She watched his face to see if his lips curled back in anger, watched his hands

84

to see if they shot out for her throat as he screamed at her that he'd known Jason MacGregor his whole life and that she was a goddamned liar.

Instead, he stepped forward and enveloped her in a hug made increasingly awkward by the difference in their heights. Not knowing what to do, she rubbed his back as asexually as possible, hoping that their mournful embrace wouldn't last long enough for the hard lump being held against her stomach to metastasize. Six or seven beats after a normal hug would have ended, this one did too.

"What you said on Facebook, it's just—it's what had to be said, you know? For Jason."

"That headcase retard's lucky the cops got to him before I did, alls I have to say about that."

"Yeah," Annick said, lifelessly. She sucked in a hard breath and leapt again. "My brother said Jason's girlfriend works here?" She tried to sip from the now-empty glass, to hide the fact that it was trembling. Sanjay had said that the young woman was a dancer, and she'd just assumed it was at the same club. Now she would find out.

"Who, Lina? She's not his girlfriend."

"Lina?" Annick asked, trying to hide her smile and the pulse throbbing the sides of her neck as though under a strobe light.

"Yeah, Lina Peng? She wasn't his girlfriend, they were just friends. How about you, you got a boyfriend?"

"Lina—is she dancing tonight?"

"Is that a yes or a no? You here with anybody?"

"No, I—yeah."

"What?"

"No, I was just—is Lina around?"

"Why the fuck you wanna see Lina?" Mike asked in a tone that was changing rapidly.

"I don't, no, I was just curious! My brother mentioned her—"

"Yeah? Who's your brother?"

Annick's head was swimming now, and she felt the last
bits of her control of the situation slipping from her grasp.
Mike raised his hand, pointing.

"Why don't you get the fuck out of here, you fat bitch?"

"Hey! There's no reason for you to talk to me like that,"
Annick said, her voice having shaken all of its falsetto flirtation, but not quite landing in as deep and steady a place
as she'd hoped.

"Oh I'm done talking, twat, and you don't want to be
around for what comes next."

"What's going on?"

Annick turned to see Philip, feeling equal thirds relief,
anger and embarrassment.

"Honey, everything's fine, just go back to the table."

"Who's this slope?"

"Slope? Are you kidding me?"

"Buddy, I wanna make you laugh, don't worry about it,
I'll pull my eyes back and stick out my teeth."

"You've got a big mouth, asshole."

"Philip, let's just get out of here."

"Buddy, I lay beatings fucking professional. Don't try me,
bitch. The fuck do you do for a living, huh? While I'm slam-
ming heads in the alley out back? Exactly. Keep walking,
bitch. You too, bitch."

Annick put her hand on Philip's shoulder. "Honey.
Let's go."

Philip smiled. "I'm a science journalist," he said.

Mike threw his head back, cackling toxically, the smok-
er's phlegm rumbling in his chest. "Holy shit, that's the most

perfect gook answer I ever heard in my life. A science journalist! Buddy. I should shitkick you on principle."

Annick and Philip turned to leave, then heard an animal roar behind them.

"Matter of fact—" Mike lunged towards them, grabbing Philip's shirt by the shoulder, getting a fistful of loose fabric without any purchase. Philip stepped forward solidly, laying a hand in the middle of Mike's chest.

"Easy. Just take it easy, alright?"

Mike grinned and slapped Philip's hand away.

"I'm not here to take it easy, slope. Your bitch picked the wrong week to poke me. I just lost my best friend. I'm ready to take some of that hurt out of your hide."

"You know, I haven't always been a science journalist."

"Philip," said Annick, grabbing his arm. "Let's go. Come on, we don't need this. Let's just go home."

"Run along home, *Daniel-san*. I'm right here when you want me."

"Daniel-san was the white character, you fucking clown."

~

Out on the street, Annick gulped for air, then let loose an equally unmeasured string of apologies. She buried her face in Philip's chest.

After a few blocks, once they knew that Mike wasn't following them, Philip stopped, stepped back and held Annick at arm's-length, by the shoulders, studying her face for some clue as to what had just happened, why they had been in that place, what she'd been talking about with that ape inside.

Annick shook her head helplessly, apologetically.

"Sweetie," she said. "I love you more than anything, and you know that. But you also knew, right from the very beginning, that there was stuff I couldn't talk to you about."

"Jesus, Annick – stuff from your practice, stuff from being a goddamned doctor. Confidentiality isn't a blanket licence to keep your loved ones completely in the dark."

Annick bit her lip again, shook her head. The whole reason she'd been in there was precisely because she was a goddamned doctor.

Wasn't it?

11

IT DIDN'T SEEM to matter at all how many times she saw it; Annick never believed that it would happen. She knew it would, intellectually, of course; just like her patients might rationally understand that their unwanted thoughts weren't reflective of their real selves, without being able to feel in their hearts that that was true. There was simply nothing intuitive about the physics of it. The long tube of a regular airplane, careening down the almost impossible length of a runway, somehow made sense even if you didn't know exactly how it worked. Contrarily, the floatplanes, snubbed and boxy, would putter along the water like little boats of no particular grace or talent before lifting almost straight up into the air, against the North Shore mountains and over Stanley Park, as though having been hoisted up out of a bathtub by a capricious, invisible giant toddler. But every time, it worked: against every instinct and gravitational pressure, dwarfed to the point of being ridiculous by the size of the water and the mountains and the trees surrounding them, the little planes would pull up at a sharp angle and for a few minutes, the baker's dozen inside would have an even closer brush against the most expensive skyline in Canada than the folks in the penthouses did.

On weekdays, Annick left too early and returned too late to see the take-offs and landings on the water's surface, restricted, as they were, to daylight hours. She missed, then, planes full of powerbroking businesspeople and members of the Legislative Assembly; people who needed to bend time in on itself, compressing the trip from Vancouver to Victoria, the provincial capital, from four hours into forty-five minutes. She only ever saw the action on weekends, from her living room on the twenty-seventh floor, when the idle rich went to and from the island for leisure-hour kicks, and didn't mind paying two or three times what it would cost to take the ferry.

Those were the kinds of thoughts that it was somewhat hypocritical to have while drinking a homemade espresso from a handmade clay mug in the aforementioned living room on the aforementioned floor, overlooking Coal Harbour— the most perfect possible name for a place that captured the dissonant collision between Vancouver's resource extraction past and wealth colony present. Whenever she felt embarrassed about the condominium, she thought of the three-bedroom Hydrostone townhouse in the not-yet-gentrified North End of Halifax where she'd grown up, and would mentally challenge whomever was questioning her current life of luxury (it was only ever her) to deny her the right to it given the way she'd come up.

Annick was doubly blessed in that she had the two things that almost nobody could find in Vancouver: a secure, pleasant place to live and a romantic partner. To be free from the need to be online checking either rental availabilities or dating profiles was to be insulated from literally the only two things that were hard about the city (Annick refused to countenance complaints about the long winter rains unless and until the complainant had had their face torn off for five endless months by the cruel winds of an actual winter, to be found almost anywhere else in the country). It made conversations with friends or coworkers or even strangers on a bus or SkyTrain almost impossible to participate in. Because she was a childless woman who'd scraped herself out from underneath her student debts and was now making what would have been technically described back home as a shitload of money, she owned a chunk of comfy skyline that was doubling in value about every six years.

But the rest of the evening, after the improvised under-cover operation at Babylon Rivers, had been as quiet and cold as the winters she'd left behind. Philip had gone to bed early, and had already left when she woke up.

And he was right: Annick wasn't a private eye, she was a cognitive behavioural therapist. It wasn't enough to sim-ply be moved by a strong concern for Sanjay's well-being; if he had cancer, she wouldn't step in to operate, and if he needed his wisdom teeth out, she wouldn't knock him unconscious and yank. Her job was in the sphere of his men-tal health, and in their sessions she could work with him to lay new neural pathways away from his unwanted thoughts and ravenous ritual compulsions, through a combination of reframing, exposure and cognitive exercises. That was all. That was the end of it.

Or, it should have been the end of it—except that one of those cognitive exercises was incriminating him in a murder he almost certainly hadn't committed. Was it really enough to say that his psychological treatment was where her responsibilities began and ended if the treatment itself was being used against him? Didn't the fact that Sanjay wasn't even willing to discuss his symptoms honestly with his own mother indicate that the very incomplete nature of their therapeutic work was now presenting a real danger to his well-being?

Annick opened the glass door onto the small patio and sat with her empty coffee, watching the boats and planes that filled Coal Harbour. She thought of the city, which somehow managed to live up to every inch of its ridiculous hype with its almost painful surplus of beauty and freedom, and she thought of Sanjay being held, alone, in jail or in the pre-trial centre, as far away from all of it as if he were on the moon, or in Manitoba.

Annick worried the knuckle of her index finger with her teeth, a bad old habit that she had more or less rid herself of except in cases of high distress. She wondered about the quality of Sanjay's defence counsel. His mother was a professor, so surely they could afford good help or maybe even call it in from friends and colleagues, but if he were getting good legal advice then why hadn't anybody asked her, the young man's psychologist, to come down and explain away a massive piece of evidence? Was Sanjay's lawyer betting everything on the strength of a negative inference, hoping that the Crown attorneys would ask for the notes and then not use them? Were they still waiting for the Crown to call her?

Or, she thought with nauseous horror, her heart sinking so far down as to take a hundred grand off the asking price of the view, was it worse than that? Was Sanjay, who couldn't level with his own mother about what he was going through, even more reticent with the stranger responsible for his legal well-being? What if the obstacle wasn't the lawyer—what if it was her guilt-eaten patient himself? What if he just couldn't bring himself to share his shame?

Annick bit back a dizzy nausea, realizing that, if that were the case, then her only chance to help him had already passed.

"Hey," said Philip, standing sweating at the door to the balcony, wearing his running gear. He pulled his headphones out of his ears, and removed the phone from the Velcro strap around his arm.

"Hey. You weren't there this morning."

"I went for a run."

"Nice," she said, wooden. "Where did you go?"

"Whole seawall, around the park."

"Nice."

They waited for each other.

"I have something I need to say to you," said Philip.

"Okay."

"I'm a journalist, you know? I'm smart too."

"I know."

"So I'm going to say something, and I know it's something you can't answer to. But I just need to say it, so that you know I know."

"Alright."

"So, stop answering."

"Yup. Sorry."

"You've been messed up for a couple of days, and I tried to retrace it, figure out when it started, and it was at lunch the other day. After I told you about the kid who murdered his roommate."

Annick's heartbeat picked up.

"They said on the news, the next day—that Facebook post? The kid, the young man, he has mental health issues. And so this is what I think: I think that kid is your patient."

Annick stopped breathing.

"I think that you think you know that he didn't do it, and it's killing you that you can't do anything without compromising his confidentiality. Don't say anything. You don't know what to do, and so last night, being you, being totally fucking crazy and being the most caring doctor in the fucking universe, you went to dig up some insane lead you thought you had."

Annick gnawed at the inside of her cheek.

"Don't say anything. Don't nod, don't shake your head. You don't have to. You never confirmed my theory. You're not going to. This is something that I figured out by myself, and I'm just thinking it out loud. Maybe there's nothing to it. You don't know. You don't tell me. But now you know: this is my working theory for what's going on. You're trying to save that kid somehow, because you know he didn't murder his room-mate. And wherever you need me to be, wherever you need me to drive, whatever you need me to do—whichever of my colleagues you need to talk to, whatever crazy nightclub or whatever you need me to go with you to, I'm just going to do it, and I'm not going to ask questions that you can't answer. And if, after you do a bunch of crazy shit, somehow that kid gets let out of jail, I'm going to look at the news on my phone, and I'm going to say, 'Huh, isn't that something—they let that kid out of jail,' and you're not going to say anything in return, and I'm just going to assume that it's because you're not interested in the story." He stopped, and looked at her. "Don't nod. Okay? Okay."

Philip's back hit the mattress before he'd had a chance to shower, and he didn't get another opportunity until very, very late in the afternoon.

12

"YOU LOOK RELAXED."

Annick smiled at Cedric over the rim of her new travel mug, a hideous ceramic tourist job that she'd picked up near the convention centre as atonement for having lost her fifth or sixth travel mug of the year when she'd left the last one in the back of the taxi. The garish white and red, festooned with maple leaves alongside the nauseating legend THE TRUE NORTH STRONG COFFEE, would be like a scarlet letter, branding her forever as a disrespectful abandoner of perfectly good caffeine receptacles. The thing was so ugly, so garish that it would simply *have* to break her streak of leaving mugs behind, a trail of them wherever she went, like bread crumbs or umbrellas. It would be easier to forget a bleeping ankle bracelet than to forget a mug so large, so lacking in wit, so singularly devoid of good taste that it bore all the aesthetic sensibility of a patriotic aneurysm.

"Yeah, for the most part, it was a pretty relaxing weekend. I'm happy it shows," Annick said, suppressing a smirk. She didn't have to worry that Cedric would see through to her Friday night cloak-and-dagger work or her gymnastic Saturday morning sexual adventures—when faced with anyone who seemed content, Cedric simply always assumed that whoever it was had finally taken his advice about mindful breathing.

"In through the nose, out through the mouth," he said with a condescending musicality, and Annick rolled her eyes and took another sip from the mug that somehow, by a dark magic of malignant aesthetic osmosis, made the coffee taste worse.

Cedric's Zen smugness wasn't entirely misplaced. After playing detective, then doctor, the weekend had wound down to a fairly manageable resting heart rate, fortifying Annick for the week ahead. She had resolved to see how Supriya and Sanjay were doing, and to start hinting strongly that it was time for Sanjay's lawyer to bring her in to set things straight. Though her heart had been in the right place, Annick felt silly about her investigation on Friday night—all she had on Lina Peng was a theory, and besides, it wasn't her job to prove who had, in fact, killed Jason MacGregor. She just had to let them know that it wasn't Sanjay.

In the office kitchen, Annick poured the contents of the tourist cup into a regular mug, and though she couldn't explain it rationally, she was convinced that somehow it tasted better again. She put another pot on to percolate and then walked up the corridor to her office, sat down at her desk and fired up her email. The first thing she noticed was a message from Supriya.

Dear Dr. Boudreau—

Most profuse apologies for my not having circled back to you earlier than this after having had to leave our dinner with such haste. Thank you for your generosity in covering the tab; despite the dolorous circum-stances in which we ate, it was clear to me that the space was a testament to the real beauty embodied in the Palestinian resistance, the injunction to live.

If she hadn't had dinner with Supriya, Annick never could have believed that this woman would naturally write or speak in anything like this language. Back home, on the East Coast, people would laugh at the phoniness when local boys came home from their first years at university in Toronto or Montréal with dictionaries between their teeth. But from Supriya, it somehow felt authentic.

After the beating to which he was subjected by fellow inmates in the jail facility on Cordova Street, it was agreed to move Sanjay to the pre-trial centre in Surrey. He was transferred there over the weekend, and I'm afraid that he spends nearly all of his time by himself. My deepest held desire is to see the strength in my son as he brushes aside this brutal and ultimately contingent misunderstanding, but it would be the purest delusion to pretend to see it—I'm afraid that his mood has deteriorated significantly, and he shows less, not more, will to fight this injustice. Guiltily, I ask myself how many of his prison guards are aware of my poetry, and whether that has exacerbated the calculated misery of his stay.

Annick was almost entirely positive that that wasn't meant as a joke.

As it happens, it would not be the only literary endeavour by our family to cause us trouble. I am afraid that I misspoke when we met, and that the so-called "murder journal" to which the authorities referred was not, in point of fact, a planted fake. With deepest embarrassment, Sanjay admitted that the notes were for a horror novel that he is planning

to write, which he was too ashamed to acknowledge earlier.

"Oh, God. Oh, no, God, please..."

It remains unclear to me why he didn't say anything
earlier, though I admit that his behaviour and tenor
have taken on such a mysterious aspect for me—even
now, I'm dialoguing with you against his wishes. He
insists that it was a mistake for me to make contact
in the first place. And though he maintains his innocence of the crime, now and again his spirit sags so
low that he tells me, "Who cares, Mom?" I'm sorry,
my eyes fill with tears as I write this. I did everything in my power to keep from him the story of the
viral social media post by Jason's friend, but one of
the guards, with typical Foucauldian/Kafkaesque
cruelty, was taunting him with it. Sanjay seems to
know that whatever happens now, nothing will be
the same. That he's been put out in front of the world
as a so-called insane man.

I've gone on so long, Annick, but of course I don't
feel that anyone but you can fully understand. You
know my sweet boy. You know that he can't possibly

That was it—Annick could see Supriya, in her mind's eye,
reaching the desperate end of the email, her distress building and, unable to continue, pressing Send before she could
erase what she'd already shared.

So Sanjay had done it—he had made the worst possible
decision, and would try to fight the charges without explaining his OCD. Maybe he didn't think explaining it would make
any difference—and maybe he was right. Annick had spent

so many years convincing her patients that nobody would think they were monsters, that she hadn't stopped to wonder if some people would.

She folded her hands over the back of her head as another thought, too painful to face sitting up straight, swooped down on her: What if she just wasn't a good enough doctor? If after three months of sessions her patient was still too ashamed to discuss his affliction with anyone, even his own mother, even if it meant a much better chance of going free, then what had she accomplished?

No. It was hard enough to come out about obsessive, intrusive thoughts to loved ones—Annick had had patients who'd needed years with her before they could explain them to their parents, the shame went so deep. But Mike Collis's imbecilic post, and the frothing, barking response to it from all the usual creeps, would-be prosecutors and hang 'em high internet moralizers, had changed things. Sanjay wasn't wrong about that. If he did get out, now, he'd be *out*—in front of everyone in the world. All at once.

"In through the nose, out through the mouth," repeated Cedric, with great warmth and friendliness, from the door to her office.

"Cedric," she answered. "Would you just fuck off?"

13

ANNICK AND CEDRIC were for the most part able to avoid each other both physically and mentally—first behaviourally, then cognitively—for the rest of the morning, which was just as well. Annick's ten a.m. appointment was a challenging one, built around a series of exposure exercises with a twenty-nine-year-old woman who had developed the sudden, crippling obsessive fear that she was a crypto-pedophile in the aftermath of her nephew's birth. In preparation, Annick had brought in a stack of old Valentine's Day cards. Her patient wasn't ready to look at photographs of real babies, so they would start, today, with controlled exposure to the winged cherubs on the valentines.

After their session, Annick turned back to her email, and saw that she'd received a reply from Philip's colleague, Bonnie Ashford, saying that she would meet her this evening, after dinner, for a drink at the Pan Pacific hotel. Annick had forgotten that she'd reached out to her on Friday evening, just before the trip to Babylon Rivers, and now felt embarrassed. Deciding that it would be more embarrassing to cancel, she decided to keep the date.

The smell of oxtail stew came into Annick's office like an olive branch. Cedric knocked on the open door with a look of contrition on his face, buttressed by confidence that he would be forgiven. The confidence likely came from the fact that he was flanked by one of Annick's very favourite people in the world, Eustace Cornwall-Manley, Cedric's wife. Eustace had been born and raised in Preston, Nova Scotia, and it was to Eustace, also, that the perfect fragrance of the oxtail stew was owed; Eustace cooked all of the meat dishes in the family, which gave Cedric a Buddhist loophole of sorts, allowing him to consume the food as an act of honouring her generosity rather than as the animal's violent sacrifice for his gluttony. Annick took Eustace into a long, warm and very necessary hug, during which Cedric held the pot of stew and rice, as well as bowls and cutlery for the three of them, serene in the assurance that the morning's brief unpleasantness had now been lost to time.

Cedric spooned out helpings while Annick and Eustace caught up.

"And how's Philip? You been back home with him yet?"

"Philip's very well, thank you. He misses you guys, he's just been snowed under completely at work. This new trade deal, I guess it has all sorts of impact on science stuff."

"'Science stuff'—that's the technical term, is it?" Eustace said, batting at Annick's forearm.

"As for back home—they're all head over heels for him, but he goes nuts back there. He says the highest thing for him to run up is the Citadel..."

"Best not do it after sundown, from what I hear—with a body like that boy's, he'll have to swat them away."

"Eustace! I think your sex-cruising information is out of date."

"Well," said Cedric tentatively, leaning forward with bowls. "Eat up, lunch'll be over before we know it."

"Look at who's mister mindfulness now," said Eustace to Annick sarcastically, and the two of them shared a laugh at Cedric's glowering expense.

"I believe, my dear," he said, regaining his full composure and knightly bearing, "that you were going to tell Annick how brilliant I was on television in her stead last week."

"I didn't have a chance to see it," Annick put in over the sound of Eustace's rolling eyes. "But I'm happy to hear it went well."

"*Ex*ceedingly," Cedric said, rewarding himself with a spoonful of gravy-soaked rice. Animal products, not to mention anything cooked, only made it past Cedric's lips once or twice a week, and when they did, they were relished. "I have sent you a link to the clip. It awaits you in your inbox. You have been relieved of your public relations duties with aplomb."

"Cedric, did you just bow?" Annick asked.

Eustace, caught off guard by a fit of laughter, had to be slapped on the back to avoid choking on oxtail.

~

The third phase of the SkyTrain line, running quietly from the airport to the downtown peninsula, had been equipped so that, unlike on the old one, cellular signals didn't cut out when the train was underground. As commuters made their way underneath the kayak-clogged waters of False Creek and towards the downtown peninsula, Annick watched Cedric's big moment on her phone, listening over earbuds. The handsome moderator lofted a fat slug of a pitch right over the plate to start him off. Somehow, either through Zen mental trickery or just the fact that he would not allow himself to be prodded, Cedric burst out of the sound byte prison in which the rest of humanity allowed themselves to be herded. He did well enough that she could reasonably expect for him to now become insufferable.

"We've become very comfortable, as a society, with snap judgments based on very little data, moments frozen in time," he'd explained patiently. "Some of us, perhaps more than others, know just how dangerous this can be. First of all, the guilt of the young suspect has not yet been proven. And even if he were found to have certainly committed the crime, we would still be faced with the difficult, one might even say impossible, job of ascertaining the role played by psychological factors."

Reaching the train's final stop, Annick followed the mass of travelling humanity up the escalators and into the larger body of the main train station. She hoped that her patients would see the video, that it would get passed around on social media—at the moment, it had been viewed 112 times. Facebook's legal department, meanwhile, had deleted Mike Collis's incendiary post, but screen-grabbed, pirate tributes were proliferating as rapidly as bacteria on a room-temperature cheese tray, and had been shared and liked tens of thousands of times.

Annick took a spot at the end of the short Starbucks lineup, ready for one last burst of caffeination to carry her through dinner and into a fully alert, fully cogent meeting with Bonnie at the hotel bar. She stepped to the counter, returning the barista's anodyne smile, then:

"Ah, *merde*."

She'd left the travel mug on the train.

~

Everything built in the 1980s had looked terrific for three years, hideous for the next twenty-five, before settling in to charming at the three-decade mark. The Pan Pacific hotel, adjacent to the five sails of the waterfront convention centre complex known as Canada Place, had been part of Vancouver's gussying up in preparation for Expo 86, the World's Fair that marked the city's audition to trade in callused hands and steel-toed boots for mani-pedis; there'd been no looking back since. The hotel's bar was the utmost in peach-coloured, Reaganomic chic, but somehow it worked. Servers in unisex and asexual vest-and-bowtie uniforms with small brass name tags gently placed glass bowls full of nut-and-rice-cracker mix in the middle of each table. A live piano player tinkled dead songs from a corner of the room.

Bonnie Ashford had already staked a table by the window overlooking Coal Harbour, and she lifted her impossibly elegant hand in a graceful wave when she saw Annick scanning the area from the main entrance. Vancouver was a city largely without Brahmins, preferring garish imported wealth to stately old money, but Bonnie Ashford was from one of the exceptional families that had been in charge since the ancient land was reconceived as a young city.

Jarrod Ashford had arrived at the place that would become Vancouver in 1886, a bootstrapping young immigrant bearing only three meagre assets: an austere Calvinist theology, an immense inheritance from his father and a perfect willingness to bring the rapacious Britishness that had worked so well in the rest of the Empire to this rainy, verdant corner of it. Jarrod Ashford became the kind of man after whom things were named, first proudly, then neutrally, then sheepishly, then not at all.

His great-great-great-granddaughter, Bonnie, became Vancouver's leading crime reporter in the years during which its underworld went genuinely international. The town had always been a North American outlier, since the mafia had never gained more than a foothold here, but in the course of the 1990s, it flowered into the weird and sporadically violent potpourri of white bikers, Hong Kong Triads and sometimes observantly religious Punjabi Sikh brawlers that it now was, and Bonnie had covered every column inch of it for the *Vancouver Chronicle* until she'd been offered an early retirement buyout during a round of newspaper layoffs, then been swept up by the CBC to the chagrin of the city's many-coloured gangsters. In accepting an award for local journalism one year, Bonnie had collected herself behind the podium with all of her patrician gravitas and said, "I ought to know Vancouver crooks pretty well—my great-great-great-grandfather was the first one, and the booty he stole was enough that it was still there to pay for my schooling."

Her silver hair was cropped nearly as short as Annick's, but she'd never stoop to brushing away phantom strands of it. As Bonnie smiled, Annick noticed what her grandfather had always called, without needing to specifically define, "*les dents des riches*"—rich people's teeth.

"You've got a tab going for that, I hope," Annick said, pointing at the sweaty, half-finished mojito on the table in front of her. "The drinks are on me tonight, please. I insist."

"Philip said you might make a scene about that. Though that's pretty much all he would say."

"I know. I apologize for the cloak and dagger. And I'm afraid I won't be doing much to clear things up. There are a few issues of confidentiality at play."

Bonnie raised a palm towards the heavens. "My dear, if there is a woman in the country to whom you owe no special pleading on protection of sources, she is me. Say no more, please. I'm cool."

Annick settled into her chair, ordered a Kahlúa and milk over ice from a handsome young waiter with girlish eyes and, when it arrived, signalled with her body language that she was ready for the conversation to begin in earnest. Bonnie immediately took the cue.

"So, what can I do for you, Doctor?"

"What can you tell me about the Babylon Rivers club?"

"Looking for a new line of work?"

"Not quite what I had in mind," Annick said, sipping her drink, and wondering whether Bonnie's shirt had been tailored recently, or whether she was one of those people who just always stayed the same size. Not all intrusive thoughts were dramatic. "I was in there a few nights ago trying to suss something out, and I don't think I went about it quite delicately enough. There's a girl who works there, and I need to talk to her."

Bonnie pursed her lips for a split second, calculating. "Well first of all, the club is a layer cake—the nightclub, the strip club and the VIP backlounge."

Annick nodded. "I sort of gathered that. The fellow I had a bit of a run-in with was a big guy, like a bouncer, but like you say, inside—at the back of the club."

"There's a muscle goon over there who recently made some headlines with a very un-PC post about mental health—may I assume, given your field, that he's the one you had it out with?"

"He's the one. Mike Collis."

"He seemed pretty broken up, from what I read. It's his friend who was killed?"

"Yeah," Annick answered. "He's—he's very pissed off. I don't try for on-the-spot diagnoses very often, because you never know what's going on with anybody until you've spent some time with them. But my first impression is that he's hurting really bad, with a lot of grief for his friend that's not coming out in very healthy ways."

"From what I understand he's just as smart as he looks, and twice as charming. But he's Lewis Blair's nephew, so they keep him around."

"Lewis Blair?"

"It's his club, his brothel in back, too. He owns a modelling school and agency on Granville, up near the bridge, and from what I can tell it's about fifty-fifty legitimate car and catalogue shoots and grooming pipeline for the stage and the parties at Babylon. I'm not speaking from experience here, of course, but this is all triangulated—"

"Triangulated?"

"Sorry—I have it from more than one source. The girls basically, from what I'm told, work a pyramid at the club, from the servers and massage girls up to the dancers and party dates. While the hoi polloi drink their watered-down booze and stare at nipples through the dry-ice fog, the back rooms run something like the Shaughnessy Heights Club, only with fewer overstuffed leather chairs, and more blow jobs. The clients there aren't treated like tricks—they don't even pay for the action, at least not directly. They party, they get laid and the girls are more or less on salary. Like an all-inclusive resort."

"Only somehow even more exploitative," Annick said, making a face.

"Cute, isn't it? Blair's stake for the club initially came from a small fortune that he'd made in film and television, but the scuttlebutt is that in around 2001, 2002, he had to take a bailout from the bikers. Only the deal worked out to everyone's advantage, and from what I understand everybody's pretty happy with the arrangement—the bikers, the sundry other interests chafing underneath them, all of them. Even though it's biker money, the VIP lounge at Babylon is treated, I'm told, as more or less neutral territory by a grab bag of the city's gangsters. So Blair, instead of finding himself the busted-out frontman for a paper business, has emerged as something of a powerbroker. Or at least the man in charge of No Man's Land."

"And yet he still finds time to be a good uncle."

"So it would seem. But if I'm not mistaken, Annick, you said you were looking for a girl?"

"One of the young women who dances there. A girl named Lina Peng?"

Bonnie shook her head, shrugging her shoulders. "I couldn't tell you anything about any of the specific dancers or working girls there. They seem to stay for a while, from what I've seen in the public area, I mean. My sense is that once they make it up the pyramid, those young women are kept fairly well, if supervised somewhat invasively."

"Their time isn't their own? I mean, like, are they being held?"

"Not quite. No, I mean—not in the sense of being locked up, passports in a desk somewhere or something."

"So one of them could get out—do something on her own time."

"I really wouldn't have any way of knowing. Do you mind if I ask who this young women is to you, Lina Peng?"

"I—I can't really say. All I know is that she was dating, or, I don't know—she was seeing a guy who worked at the club as a doorman," Annick said. "The kid who got killed, Jason MacGregor."

"Oh," Bonnie said, then squinted, then smiled. Annick could tell that she wanted to ask how Annick could possibly enter into that equation, then remembered her promise not to do any prodding.

"So, their boss, the asshole's uncle, Lewis Blair. He's a bad guy?"

"At the very least, he has all the bad guys' phone numbers," Bonnie said, stirring the ice left in the last sips of her mojito with her straw. "A few years back, for instance, one of Blair's neighbours, who had recently taken an interest in whose trees overhung whose property lines, ended up in the emergency room."

Annick and Bonnie sat for a few minutes longer, finishing their drinks, gossiping about shared acquaintances in the tiny community of Vancouver media. Annick stood when they were finished and laid two twenties on the table, because she was garish new money, and Bonnie was stately enough not to widen her eyes at the overkill tip. The two women rose from their seats, pecked each other's cheeks, and Annick's gratitude was tamped down by Bonnie's repeated insistence that it was nothing.

"You guys are just down on the water here, aren't you?" Bonnie asked.

"That's right."

"So are you just headed home then?"

"Yup. One quick stop first."

~

Three hours later, Annick was sitting at one of the fibreglass tables of Tides, a franchise in the same chain of coffee shops as sold the tortilla samosas in the foyer of her office building. This location, contrarily, was one street over from Babylon Rivers, sharing an alleyway with the club, and as the scattering of dedicated summer students pecked at the blue glow of laptops around her, the alley was what Annick had been watching intently. Every twenty minutes or so, for the last hour and a half, one or another superlatively beauti-ful young woman exited from the second floor, and was escorted by a squat young man into a waiting taxi. Without wanting to admit to racial profiling, Annick was neverthe-less fairly certain that she had yet to see anyone who could be a "Lina Peng."

At 1:54 a.m., as she finished punching out another text promising Philip that she would be home soon, Annick's eye was caught by a bright blue cab pulling into the lane. The door on the second floor opened to release the same squat man and, this time, a young Chinese woman with a shim-mering beauty so pronounced that even from this distance, it felt fragile. Lina Peng, if this was her, was long and lithe, with two thick, shining curtains of black hair framing what seemed, even from a distance, to be a beautiful, porcelain face. Her thin body was wrapped in a soft summer jacket. Before even knowing if this was Lina, Annick found her-self trying to imagine whether this chimera could take a life. In some ways it seemed impossible—but the most distinct impression given by this particular beauty was that there was nothing it couldn't do.

Just before the woman was relayed into the back seat of the cab, the door on the second storey was flung open again. A large, dark figure was silhouetted for a second in the yel-low light, calling out something muffled, stopping both the girl and her bodyguard in their tracks. Mike Collis ran quickly down the stairs, relieving the other man and sending him back into the club. Mike took the girl by the inside of her arm and yanked her a few feet away from the prying ears of the cabbie.

Annick had an even weaker angle on the dialogue than the cab driver did, but there was no soundtrack necessary to determine that these were two people who knew each other well, and didn't like each other at all. The face of the beautiful girl would ricochet between fright and strident self-possession, and though Collis clearly dominated the physical field, the angry dialogue was not one-way. Then Mike's index finger came so close to the woman's face that Annick wondered if she didn't have a responsibility to phone the police, when just as suddenly the woman broke away from the conversation entirely, slipping into the cab, which started immediately down the alley despite Mike's angrily swatting the side of it.

Annick poured the last dregs of her cold decaf down her throat as Mike ascended the stairs and disappeared.

Walking the seawall back to the condo, Annick was grateful for the breeze on her face. Vancouver's night-time summer air, coming off the surface of the water, was a pleasure ecstatic enough to explain at least part of the housing prices.

Annick went back over her theory, and it seemed to be at the very least still plausible, and if anything more likely. She knew that Lina and Jason had a long history of angry break-ups and make-ups; now Annick knew as well that Jason's grief-stricken best friend was furious with her. She recalled how he'd spat her name on Friday, going so far as to deny that she had been Jason's girlfriend. Maybe even the cave-man was starting to see that there might be some holes in the Crazy Roommate Slasher hypothesis. Not that he could take it back now that he'd stepped up onto the soapbox and growled it to the world.

But there still wasn't enough to take to the police. Annick knew that no one was looking into the girlfriend since, as far as they were concerned, they already had their guy. An anonymous tip wouldn't even roust anybody from their desk.

She shook her head and laughed bleakly, realizing that she was having the same desperate thought as every creep in the front row at the strip club: How can I get that girl to talk to me?

14

ANNICK HAD ALWAYS been pretty, with the exception of the hump of early teenage years when nobody was except for a chosen few. And though she had grown up in a time when only skeletal hints at femininity had dominated the covers of magazines, and online porn engines hadn't yet made clear that the spectrum of human desire was far broader than anyone had been told, she'd still suspected that there were boys who preferred her more substantial frame—what the internet, in its wisdom, had later dubbed *thiccness*, and saw that it was good.

To be envious of models and movie stars for their looks had never made any sense to Annick. Sure, it was inevitable to size oneself up against friends and family, colleagues and strangers riding the same train; she was a human being. But when people watched Sidney Crosby or LeBron James playing sports, were they *envious* of them? Maybe on some distant, abstract level, but for the most part their arbitrary endowments from the fates were of such a qualitatively different stuff that it acted as a leveller, allowing knots of otherwise competitive men to relax around each other and marvel without guile or anxiety.

So as she flipped through the large pages of the catalogue in her lap, Annick didn't feel a self-consciousness about her thirty-five years, or the fleshiness of her arms, or the fact that she didn't have skin the perfect colour of chilled *crème caramel*. Instead, she just marvelled at what some people's faces could look like.

The reception area of the Agar Modelling Agency & School was as austere as a model's lunch, done in the icy tones of an advertisement for vodka. Annick had walked up the steep wooden staircase away from the noise and heat of Granville Street, approached the young woman behind the reception desk and told her the exact truth: that she was a therapist charged with the responsibility of producing new brochures for her office, and that she would like to look at a catalogue of Agar models. If it seemed that these two statements were causally linked, that was based entirely on assumptions made by the receptionist.

Annick had been handed a wide, thick catalogue with a two-page spread for each of the models, with the verso page featuring a large, intimate colour headshot, and the recto page featuring three full-body poses as well as the name and statistics of the model. There didn't seem to be any particular order to the listings, and so Annick simply sat, awkwardly balancing the catalogue on her lap, and turned the pages until she came to the headshot that, even among the others, slapped the viewer like a perfumed glove.

The hair like a waterfall done in India ink, the slightly crooked face whose asymmetry gave the impression of being wrought precisely by God's hands, its imperfections bespoke and therefore not flaws at all, stared out from the large, unsmiling headshot. There was only one photo in which she was smiling, balanced delicately on a nice-looking and probably not particularly comfortable piece of Nordic furniture. Five feet, nine inches tall, 116 pounds—and, yes, her name was Lina Peng. Annick took a deep breath.

The ethics that defined her psychological practice were fairly clearly laid out, and her adherence to them helped give Annick's life shape and purpose. The ethics that governed her broader interactions as an individual within society as a whole were necessarily cloudier, but Annick was conscious of the fact that, by more or less anybody's standards, what she was about to do was a breach of them. She exhaled.

Crossing the room back to the front desk, Annick received a broad smile from the receptionist, and she returned it. She turned the ungainly catalogue around on the counter and pointed.

"She's gorgeous," she said.

"Oh my God, they all are."

"Right? But I think she'd be great for the brochure." Annick suddenly felt very self-conscious, and wanted a reason for the choice beyond just the model's sexual desirability. "We treat a lot of patients for depression, and other anxiety disorders, and so we may not decide to go with a smiling image on the brochure. She looks great without smiling, too, which may be the way we want to go."

The receptionist gave an understanding nod. "Yeah, Lina's great."

"When would be her first availability?"

"Let me just check," answered the receptionist, tapping at the keyboard. "I know it's soon, but it actually looks like she has some time Wednesday afternoon."

"Tomorrow? That would be perfect, thank you."

"And where's the shoot?"

"Oh," said Annick. "Well, actually, I was hoping—I thought it would be best, if it's okay, to meet first?"

"Oh," said the receptionist. Trying unsuccessfully to maintain her look of professional politeness against creeping confusion. "Um, why?"

It was an excellent question.

"Yeah, no. We just—because of the treatment philoso-phy at our clinic, we try to... It's just very important to always—" The receptionist's face was turning to a sterner dimension of disapproval, and Annick could tell that, if she were a man, Lina's Wednesday slot would have sud-denly filled magically with another commitment. She found the gravitas which she normally reserved for conference presentations. "Cognitive behavioural therapy is used to treat very challenging mental illnesses, some of which are incredibly stigmatized. With any of our clinic's front-facing work, we feel it's very important that anyone we partner with gets a sense of what we're doing, and why we do it." She hadn't really said anything, but she had said it with confidence—even used the obnoxious "front-facing"—and she could tell that she had turned the receptionist slightly back on-side. "Obviously, we would pay the booking rate for that time as well. And I could just meet Ms. Peng for a coffee downstairs tomorrow afternoon."

Having relinquished the suspicion that this was any weird sex thing, the receptionist had by now moved on to a state of chilling indifference. "So, Wednesday at one p.m., would that work?"

"That would be great, yes, thank you—I can meet her at the Starbucks next to the Vogue?" The art deco theatre was visible from the Agar reception area.

"Okay, consider it confirmed."

"Great, thank you," Annick answered, with maybe too much relief. She skittered over to the door, down the steep and creaking staircase, and back out into the loud sunni-ness of Granville Street. She squinted into the glare, reached into her purse and scooped out a pair of chunky sunglasses, slipping them on. She had time before she had to see any patients; she could cross False Creek by foot, then catch a cab on the other side.

Annick started across the Granville Street Bridge, the billion-dollar skyline of a thousand car commercials at her back. She stared out past the Burrard Bridge, like the Vogue and City Hall one of the city's rare instances of art deco, and into the wide green-blue of English Bay. She looked down and saw Granville Island, which would even today, in the middle of the putative workweek, be teeming with summer crowds, tourists throwing bread crumbs to pigeons in violation of signs prohibiting same, local stage actors on break from rehearsing American plays. She watched seagulls and crows, nodded smiles at dog-walkers and felt the wind blow hard against her face. This is what it is to be alive.

Annick had thought so much about Sanjay that she had barely considered Jason MacGregor, placed beyond the possibility of ever again experiencing a breeze across the span of the Granville Street Bridge. She considered how little she knew about the man—thrown into an uncomfortable intimacy with Sanjay, a perfect stranger, by a too-low rental vacancy rate and the fates of online listings; she knew that he did not keep a clean house, that he prepared protein-heavy meals without much consideration of spreading bacteria; she knew that he was big and tough enough to work the door at a nightclub that was also a strip joint and a high-end brothel. All that she knew about his tastes were that they ran to the frenetic drumming and simple chord progressions of early West Coast hardcore. She knew that he and his girlfriend had had a tumultuous relationship; had fought so frequently, and so viciously, that her sensitive patient had found it necessary to block up his ears. Other than that, all she knew was that he had been violently killed, slashed across the throat, and that was the end of him. Sanjay had at least a chance to walk these streets again; Jason was gone. He probably wasn't someone she would have particularly liked. But the world was full of people who didn't share her interests or her inclinations, and each of them had the right to go on drawing breath. Jason MacGregor should have gone on for decades as a person with whom, just barely, she was sharing a planet, a country, a city.

Annick tried and failed to imagine Lina Peng's perfect face twisted in a rictus of rage, screaming loudly enough that Sanjay couldn't bear the noise. Rage seemed almost too human an emotion for a countenance so Platonic; it didn't feel like she'd been built to process the same base emotions as other people had. But she had yelled at Mike, in the alley, and it hadn't been pretty. Which was to be expected if she thought that he suspected her.

But she had fought with Jason, and Annick was proceeding from the assumption that she had done more than that: that she had murdered him, and left the hapless roommate, already weighed down by his own troubles, to wear it. Annick began to think of the meeting, and how she would go about prying Lina open. She had never interrogated a suspect, but she was nevertheless an expert in reading where people were at—spotting what deficit there might be between what they were saying and what they were feeling—and getting them to share the things that were burdening them, sometimes even if they thought they didn't want to. She thought again about the line between her professional ethics and her personal morality as she realized she was considering, now explicitly, using the skills she'd developed for therapeutic treatment in order to accomplish something else.

She had been circling what she was feeling, refusing to name it, but it came into focus too clearly for her to ignore: she was terrified. Still, she would do it. For Sanjay. And for Jason.

15

"DID YOU—HAVE YOU seen that Facebook post by that guy? The one everybody's talking about?"

It had rained earlier in the afternoon, and the summer downpour had left Vancouver with the mix of relief and disappointment that it always did. At the moment, the raindrops seemed to hang in the air, clinging to some invisible scaffolding while the cars on the road took longer and longer to brake on surfaces slick with rehydrated oil fumes. On an afternoon like this, it seemed impossible that the city smelled any different than it had when the rainforest was still standing; an overwhelming organic smell, humid and leafy, like something dying and something being born. In these instances, the mood of the entire city changed at once, and fractured—with thousands of people hunched over, holding migraines between their fingers, and thousands of people saying, "About time, eh?" and thousands of people saying, "Can you believe people are already complaining about it?" and the rest of them feeling the shameful pleasure of release from the moral injunction to go outside. People in Vancouver never stopped saying how you could hike, ski and swim all in the same day—they always failed to mention, though, that nobody wanted to.

Three years ago, Dr. Boudreau had run a therapeutic course with David, a patient who'd had one of the worst cases of health anxiety—what they used to call "hypochondria"— that she'd ever come across. He had become so intent on palpating his glands, for instance, that he had left deep purple bruises along his jawline, so that it looked as though he had escaped an àttempted strangulation. They had worked together, doing exposure and laying out certain ground rules—he was entirely forbidden from googling symptoms; he would only go to the doctor in the case of acute or worsening symptoms; he would get his wife to read the list of side effects on any new medications and watch for them in him, rather than his reading them and then immediately imagining that they were presenting—and within a few months, David was well within the range of normal behaviour.

But when he had become a father, David had experienced a tremendous amount of slippage, not for himself but projected onto his baby daughter. He had found it much harder to locate the broad sweet spot of reasonable behaviour when it came to worrying about fevers or rashes or cuts affecting his little girl. David and his Dr. Boudreau were now in the fifth week of a refresher course, and he was doing well. Now he wanted to know what she thought of The Facebook Post.

The Facebook Post had never been far from the surface of any conversation she'd had, with either colleagues or patients, since it went up, then was nominally taken down, before being reborn as an unstoppable, undead meme. The grieving Mike Collis—who, Annick now believed, realized he may have fingered the wrong person for the murder of his best friend—had become a telling-it-like-it-is folk hero. The story he had laid out, of an innocent man disturbed by his crazy roommate's bizarre and manic behaviour, but told by his heartless landlords that they had no legal recourse except to leave him be, was being conflated with all other manner of prejudice and bigotry. *Yeah, and why should my daughter have to share her school washroom with a boy just because he thinks he's a girl*, they said, needing only the most tenuous connection by analogy, or abandoning any logical tendril, however threadbare, and taking off entirely into space: *Yeah, and why should we be ashamed of our country's first prime minister just because he wasn't politically correct.* There were blog posts in a more progressive academic mould, too, which made a strong disavowal of any "ableist" prejudice against people suffering from mental illness, before reasserting the need to honour intuitive feelings of unease around "creepy men." All in all, as in most things, Annick found the level of discourse to be profoundly stupid and depressing.

Her colleagues had seemed, for the first few days, to be dumbstruck: they had genuinely thought that, after all the hashtag campaigns and awareness weeks sponsored by cellphone companies to destigmatize mental illness, we just *had* to be further along than this, as a society. Among her patients, Dr. Boudreau had noticed a shrinking, a reticence—some of them, whom it had taken months and years to convince that they were okay, now seemed to wonder if they could take her word for it, let alone their own.

David was her last appointment of the evening, and though she tried to find a more elevated, professional language in which to respond to his question, she just couldn't.

"That guy is a completely shitheaded fucking asshole."

David giggled conspiratorially, but also with what seemed like relief. "Yeah, I mean—free speech though, I guess?"

"Please—you will never find a bigger free speech absolutist than me. I'm French, remember, we're the ones who take it too far. But libel has never been protected speech. He's convicting that young man, when he's innocent until proven guilty."

"Yeah. But it looks bad though, doesn't it?"

"Well, that's why I'm glad we have lawyers and judges and juries who've been given strict evaluative criteria to decide, rather than taking a bloody internet referendum on how people *feel* every time." She could see from David's face that she had lost her cool, and smiled. "But I don't really have any opinion one way or the other."

David laughed. "I can see that."

"Think about how much time you and I have spent in this office talking about how dangerous it can be to trust feelings. How many times did you just *know* that you were dying, because you could feel it?"

"Every time."

"Exactly."

As Dr. Boudreau walked David out into the reception area to lock up, she saw Supriya sitting, pinched and pale grey, in one of the chairs by the entrance. She saw David out and locked the door behind him.

"Supriya, are you okay?"

"My son—" she said, then broke off under a rush of tears. Instinctively, Annick took her into her arms, kneeling in front of her chair and letting Supriya pour herself onto her shoulders.

"Are we—" Supriya said, suddenly snapping alert. Annick nodded.

"Everybody is gone for the day. There's nobody else here. Even Cedric is gone."

"Who?"

"Sorry, nobody. Don't worry about it. What can I do?" Supriya burst back into tears.

Annick sat herself in the chair next to her, and let her soak the sleeveless blue silk top that she was, now, likely wearing for the very last time. They sat, and Supriya cried, for what must have been five minutes. It was as if, having held herself ramrod rigid for a week, Supriya had snapped in Annick's embrace. All of it, having been deferred, came now.

Sniffling, Supriya reached into her purse and produced a sealed envelope.

"He made me promise to get you to sign it, that it was still sealed when I gave it to you." Annick nodded, but couldn't contain her excitement at finally having word directly from Sanjay. She ripped the envelope as though famished.

Dear Dr. Boudreau—

My mother has promised to give you this without reading it herself, and I'm begging you not to share the contents with her. Please.

I'm so sorry that I didn't reach out myself before now, except sending my mom to you right after. I needed to tell you that I didn't do it. For some reason that was like the most important thing in that moment. Now of course I realize that obviously you were the only one who would know that I didn't. Everybody else is sure that I did.

This is probably stupid or whatever but I just have to say it. Don't feel guilty because you got me to do the journal. I think it became like a new compulsion for me, I don't know. I kept writing it all down not because you told me to but because if I wrote them, it was like I could tell myself that it was okay not to think about them or do the rituals to get rid of them. Like in a weird way that I was holding myself responsible, keeping a log of the evidence that I could go back to later and punish myself.

I was lying in my room the whole time it happened, with those stupid headphones on. I couldn't hear anything. I was listening to music and lying down because I'd had such a bad attack of thoughts. I was trying to do like you said, trying to sit with it. But after a while my hands felt so dirty and I just went into the bathroom and started washing right up to the elbows, and I didn't even hear the cops come in.

The first couple of days I lost all sense of reality. There were times when I started to wonder if maybe I actually had done it, because it just didn't feel like I had any solid ground to stand on at all. It's the craziest I've ever felt. I just froze. I couldn't tell the lawyer about my OCD. It didn't even feel like that's what it was. It felt like I was hallucinating, nothing felt real. I told my mom the least possible I could get away with. I panicked and I told them my journal was notes for a horror book. So fucking dumb.

When the other prisoners beat me up, all I could feel was relief. It was like I was finally being punished for the thoughts. I know you are a good doctor and please don't take this the wrong way at all but when those guys beat the shit out of me, it was like they saw what I could never make you see. That this is the real me, that I am evil. If there is one thing I know for sure to be true, it's that I am evil. You looked for the good in me but I just don't think it was there.

When I saw that post from Jason's friend, I realized that it was probably all true. Jason had caught me doing the compulsions a few times, saw me with the hand washing and everything, and he knew I was crazy. He told me I was crazy, that I was creeping him out. It totally makes sense that he would've talked to the landlords. It seems weird that they would say that about my human rights or whatever, but maybe they were smarter than I thought. Or maybe that was just them blowing him off. We could never get them to fix a damn thing in our unit, and Jason used to complain that once they had found me to take the second room downstairs, they'd checked out completely.

I know it seems like the worst thing, to have a post like that go out, but it made me feel the same relief as the beating. People finally know what's in me. The thoughts are me—I think therefore I am, right?

You have been a good doctor and you have been kind to me, I think probably because you never saw the real me. The things you say about the thoughts may be true of other patients, but you are wrong about me, I'm sorry.

With these thoughts running through my mind day and night, it is only a matter of time before I snap and do something crazy. The way things have worked out, I feel like the universe is saving everybody from me before I do something that I regret. I don't want to be a danger to anyone. I don't want to hurt the people I love.

I didn't kill Jason. But I am going to tell them that I did.

Please destroy this letter, and sign the envelope that you're the only one who read it. I'm trusting you.

Sanjay

Annick Boudreau was not a crier.

One of the family's favourite bits of lore, told and retold until the anecdote had calluses, concerned a family camping trip in the New Brunswick bush in the summer that Annick turned four, when her cousin Guillaume—himself only nine, and in the midst of a tantrum—had tossed a long-handled axe which landed, happily flat side down, onto her bare foot. Her uncle Yvan, Guillaume's father, had lunged in their direction, whether to scoop up Annick or to smack Guillaume she couldn't say, and Guillaume had immediately started screaming, "*Je m'excuse, cousine!*" but Annick had stunned the family into granting him amnesty by offering nothing more than a bemused look, followed by a giggle. The grown-ups had assumed that the axe head must not have hit her as hard as they'd thought—but the following morning, the top of her foot was bruised as black as its dirt-stained sole. "*Maudit qu'elle est* tough, *ta cousine,*" Yvan had said, gobsmacked, and she'd never outgrown the reputation in the family. Lost boyfriends, near run-ins with unintended motherhood—each left their mark, but seldom did they occasion any tears.

It didn't come from any feelings of contempt for, or superiority to, those who did cry. Siblings and cousins and friends, male or female, knew early on that Annick's shoulder was a soft patch in an otherwise rough world; that she would offer comfort and succour to those who wept, whatever the reason was for it, and this pre-therapeutic instinct was something that she took with her from the Acadian Atlantic to school in Montréal, where she sopped up innumerable undergraduate tears on dorm room floors and apartment couches. In her work at the clinic, a day seldom passed without Annick being there as someone's floodgates opened up, and she was always prepared with a box of tissues, with a face that promised that it was alright. She just wasn't a crier herself.

Which is why at first, standing in the reception area, reading Sanjay's letter to herself while Supriya watched her face for reactions, Annick hadn't even recognized that it was starting. The desperate gravity of the missive pulled her in so crushingly that she couldn't feel her eyes stinging or the muscles trembling in her face, and when the first splashes hit the paper, she had actually looked up at the ceiling.

"Are you alright?" Supriya had asked with angry concern. "What does he say?"

Feeling as dizzy and derealized as any of her panic disorder patients in the midst of an attack, Annick had started by mutely waving Supriya off, shaking her head, *No*, as though she could pretend that it wasn't happening.

"I'm fine, I'm sorry, Supriya. It's been a very long day." Supriya eyed her skeptically. "In a very long week," she added, taking a deep breath and managing to stop the waterworks.

"But what does my son say, that you would react this way? Don't I have a right to know? I am the boy's mother, Dr. Boudreau."

Annick shook her head, grateful for having been addressed by her professional title. "I'm so sorry, Dr. Desai. I really can't share it without Sanjay's permission. I know that to you he's your boy, but in this office he is a grown man, he's my patient, and the protection of his confidentiality is one of my primary responsibilities."

"Well, this is outrageous," Supriya answered with as much resignation as chagrin. Annick reached out to touch her arm, and Supriya allowed her to.

"Supriya, the entire situation—it's like nothing I've ever been through, been a part of. And I know I'm not going through a fraction of what you and Sanjay are feeling." Annick watched Supriya's eyes as they softened into a focus outside of the room. Her anger was dissolving visibly. Annick guided her to one of the seats, pouring her a glass of water from the cooler. "I want you just to sit here for a second, have a glass of water, and I'm just going to write Sanjay a message for you to take back to him. Can you do that for me?"

Supriya nodded.

"Thank you. I will be right back, okay?" Annick could hear her voice crashing over solicitousness and now in danger of falling into condescension. She backed out of the foyer, the letter from her patient beginning to shake with her hand, and she was positive that she wouldn't make it down the short corridor before her knees buckled.

With the door to her office closed behind her, she squeezed her eyes as though wringing the tears out of them, screaming silently into her palm. Then she sat at her desk, and she typed.

Dear Sanjay—

No.

For some time, she couldn't think of anything else to add. Then, the only non-bathetic response she could muster came from anger, from professional indignation, and so she gave it vent.

I need you to understand that I have a much more accurate understanding than you do of what goes through your mind. You are stuck inside of something you've never seen the outside of, and I've been studying it my entire life. I've seen it from every angle. I've helped dozens, maybe more, people out of it. And I need for you to listen to me as your doctor: YOU DID NOT DO ANYTHING WRONG. THERE IS NOTHING EVIL IN YOU. THERE IS NO DANGER THAT YOU REPRESENT, AND SACRIFICING YOURSELF IN THIS WAY PROTECTS NO ONE. NO ONE, SANJAY.

There is a world out there that understands nothing at all about OCD, and Sanjay, I say this with as much kindness as I can: right now, you are a part of that world. You're just as wrong as every one of those imbeciles on Facebook.

I need for you to tell your lawyer to bring me in. You don't have to tell them why if you don't want to, I can explain the entire thing. You don't have to tell your mother, although Sanjay, she loves you, and she is a brilliant woman, and she will understand. Better than you do.

It's possible that your lawyer will tell you that if he brings me into the situation, they can subpoena my notes. We can cross that bridge when we get to it, I will fight like fucking hell for your privacy, but I also wouldn't be saying this if I didn't think that my clinical notes from our sessions would absolve you completely. Tell your lawyer that I said that. Tell him that the more rocks they turn over, the less they are going to have on you. Because you didn't do it.

The very last thing I told you, Sanjay, was that you are not a monster, you are not a killer. It was so obvious to me that I considered your even having to ask it to be counterproductive, reassurance-seeking behaviour. But I will tell it to anyone who asks, if you give me the right to.

Don't do this. Don't do this. For you, for your mother. For Jason, your asshole roommate whose actual killer is still loose. For me.

Just tell your lawyer to bring me in. Give me the chance to explain all this. Let me continue my work.

Dr. Boudreau

Annick walked back to the reception area in a daze. Mechanically, she slipped the folded letter into an envelope and handed it to Supriya, who was now standing, leaning on the front counter.

"I need you to get this to him." Annick spoke in a voice so raw that Supriya simply nodded. "Can you get this to him?"

"Yes."

"When?"

"As soon as I can—this evening. I'll call the lawyer, pass it to him, he can give it to Sanjay."

"Okay."

"Dr. Boudreau, I am ground down. They are killing my child, and I have no one. What are you prepared to do?"

"Everything that I possibly can. But he's the only one who can make it happen. Please, please get him that letter."

"Alright." Supriya nodded, curtly, and turned to walk out. Annick ran to the door before it closed and shouted down the hallway.

"Let me know when he gets it, please!"

"Yes. I will." Supriya turned to call the elevator and didn't turn back.

Annick closed the door to the clinic, locked it and collapsed into one of the chairs in the waiting area. Her head pounded as though her first tears in decades had left her completely dehydrated, and she stood and poured herself small, wax-paper cup of water after small, wax-paper cup of water, hugging the tank for support.

After her sixth cup, she realized that she hadn't sealed the envelope.

Freud said that there was no such thing as accidents, that accidents were just the acting out of forbidden desires, sublimated by the super-ego. In this reading—this archaic, disproven, well-out-of-favour reading—Annick hadn't innocently forgotten to seal the envelope, but had set out precisely to give Supriya an insight that she was otherwise bound not to share; in this reading, she was flailing at her lowest, most desolate and destroyed moment, trying to recruit an ally. In this reading, Annick wanted to send the message to Supriya that her son was not only decent and innocent, but that he was in trouble much worse than he had to be in, and that if she could convince him to only let his doctor help them, then they all had a chance.

Annick Boudreau thought Sigmund Freud was full of shit.

But Freud might call that disavowal.

~

"Bonjour toi."

"Allo, Pa. J'pensais à toi."

"Ah *oui*? And what did I do to have you thinking of me?" asked Roméo.

"Well, I'm calling from the office—"

"Sure, sure. I've heard that one before. Tell me another one."

"Non, je te jure, Papa—I promise. This time I'm really calling from the office."

"You can't prove it. You're like that little boy with his wolf."

"You'll have to believe me."

"You didn't listen to the story then, eh? That's the whole moral, the wolf really does come, and it's too late, nobody believe him. *Tant pis pour toi, le petit menteur. Ou la petite menteuse*," he said, and she could hear her father grinning, giving both the masculine and the feminine for "liar." She sighed. She didn't have time to explain to her father that she spent all day, every day, dealing with flight-or-fight responses on the fritz, imperfect and misfiring clusters of instincts handed down from a time when wolves actually did present an immediate danger to a large percentage of the population. But these were different times; in Annick's line of work, she'd come to learn that there never really was a wolf.

"*Non*, Roméo—I called because I had a patient today, made me think of you."

"I thought you tell me all the time, you can't talk to me about your patients anyway."

"I'm not allowed to tell you their names, Papa, any recognizable features. I can speak in generalities."

"Like the Pope."

"I can tell Maman is out; you said that above a whisper."

"You know Maman is out because I answered the phone," he said, giggling. Annick laughed too, but she couldn't keep herself from scanning the sound of his laughter for the exhaustion that her mother had reported. The idea of her father heavy-lidded, slow to rise, was like the hiss of water pouring onto the white ashes of a bonfire. It both undermined and exaggerated the memories of what came before. But she hadn't imagined it, she was sure; her father leaning into his fiddle at parties, tickling her under the jaw in the middle of Sunday Mass, then pretending to be angry when Thérèse noticed her laughing—he *had* lived. "She's out late, who knows where. Must be with her boyfriend."

"It was bound to happen."

"So what did this patient do to make you think of me? He had delusions of grandeur, about his kid?"

"The patient suffers from health anxiety."

"'Health anxiety'—*c'est quoi*? Like health food? An anxiety that's better for you? He should bottle it, all your neighbours in Vancouver will line up to buy it."

"I never said the patient was a 'he.' Hypochondria, Papa. Always in a panic about their health."

"Ah, okay, I can see why you thought of me."

"*Très drôle*. In fact, I was thinking about how nice it would be if the two of you could cancel each other out."

"That's a nice thing to say."

Annick laughed in the perfect and unique combination of frustration and adoration with which daughters can laugh at their fathers. "Don't be so sensitive. I meant, if only the two of you could crash together, and each leave the collision as a sensible person with a perfectly constructive level of interest in their own personal health."

"Ah."

"My patient would leave worrying much, much less—pay far fewer visits to the doctor, the emergency room..."

"I've heard about those..."

"And *you*. You would leave as someone who would at least take his family's love seriously enough to go and see about—"

"*Non, non, non. Ça là, c'est trop.* You go too far. That's blackmail."

"Papa, if you're tired all the time—"

"I'm not tired, goddamn, I'm old!"

"You're not old."

"Not in Vancouver, *non*. But in the real world, *oui*, I am old."

"To be tired all the time," Annick continued, barrelling through his defences, "and to be having trouble in the bathroom consistently, and to have—to have blood, in your stools—"

"And who sends you these updates on my shits, *maudit hell?*" he yelled. There was no more playful parrying or thrusting. He would dig his Acadian heels into the dirt, the heels of a man raised from the beginning to believe that there was no greater human attribute than spiteful stubbornness. But she, too, was in the family line.

"Papa, what you're describing—"

"I never described to you a goddamn thing!"

"Your symptoms add up badly. They don't look good together, like that."

"And aren't you the little girl who won't stop telling us she's not that kind of doctor?"

"Papa, it could be *cancer.*"

They each stopped talking, caught their breath. They offered each other, and themselves, a chance to step down from the heights. When the conversation resumed, it was more muted, almost anglophone in the washed-out tones of its passions.

"It's not cancer," said Roméo.

"And how do you know?"

"God gave it to my granddaughter. He's not going to stick it on me. It would be cruel."

Annick closed her eyes and rubbed her thumb in the space between her eyebrows. "God doesn't give people cancer, Papa."

"*Non?*"

"No. He gives them little girls who love them, wives who love them—and get them to go see a doctor."

They sat breathing together, separated by the whole continent, brought back together with each inhalation, exhalation. Somewhere, Cedric was smiling smugly.

"*S'il te plaît*, Papa. Go see Dr. Breaux. For me? For Maman?"

"I'll tell Maman you called."

"Papa..."

"I'll call Dr. Breaux."

"*Merci.*"

Annick looked at the phone, running her finger along the receiver, making a face she'd probably started making when she was a child, and only dusted off for the moments when one or both of her parents broke her heart.

For all the promises, she had lied to her father. It hadn't been David who had made her think to call Roméo. It had been Sanjay. And Supriya. And the responsibility that came from the cosmic accident of being somebody's kin in a terrifying and chaotic, a fallen, world. A place where very bad things happened, even to people who came as close as it was possible to being good.

16

THE STARBUCKS LOOKED like any other Starbucks, and contained roughly the same number of people. By the evening, even on a weeknight, the Smithe Street windows would face out onto the sophisticated beige and silver patrons of the Vancouver Symphony Orchestra, while the Granville Street windows would act as something like the glass of a terrarium showcasing the city's thriving margarita-vomiting scene. But in the middle of the afternoon, outdoors was a downtown grab bag of every and any type of pedestrian, while inside the store it was the standard-issue demographic of youngish men and women with laptops but no offices, and ESL students conspiring to produce the next generation of half-Korean, half-Brazilian babies.

Annick sucked a tall flat white through the hole in her plastic cup, once more quietly conceding to the multinational corporation that their coffee wasn't as bad as she'd have liked it to be, ideologically. She had chosen a table in one of the corners where the wall met a Smithe Street window, and was seated with her back to the corner as she was given to understand, from film and television, that was the place where she was supposed to sit. She brushed a phantom strand of hair out from her face and behind her ear.

She was running down the list of things she would look for to push her towards something like certainty that it had been Lina who'd killed Jason. The real murderer had bled on the scene, so there would still be a cut—maybe bruising from the scuffle. She would float the same story that she had used with Mike, that she'd known Jason growing up, and see what her reaction was. Besides that, it wasn't clear what she could do, beyond what she did for a living: let people know, via a thousand tiny cues of voice and body, that they could and should take her into their confidence.

When it finally happened, Lina's entrance threw off the whole balance of the room. Like the very slight turn at the end of her jaw, the whole energy of the café seemed to bend, as though her beauty brought everyone else into its orbit. Even without looking at her, the men, the women in the room, everyone seemed at least to notice that now things were somehow different. She was several steps down in glamour today from both the portfolio shots and her alleyway argument with Mike, but it was just as if a lampshade had been taken off of a light. Her hair was piled in an intricate lattice-work of bobby pins, and she wore high-end sweatpants and a long-sleeved turtleneck, which seemed out of place given the heat from the returned power of the summer sun. Annick stood and smiled, and Lina gave her a look of acknowledgement without greeting or warmth, and joined her at the table.

"Hi, Lina? I'm Annick, Dr. Boudreau, from the West Coast CBT Clinic."

Lina nodded, and sat. The graceful posture of her walking died in the chair, her shoulders hunching down. Annick noticed that Lina's eyes were glassy, her face impassive. She tried giving her a smile.

"Can I get you anything to eat or drink?"

"I'm fine."

"Right," Annick said, sitting. "Okay. Well, first of all, I want to thank you for meeting with me. Obviously we're going to pay you for your time here, but I know that a pre-shoot meeting like this isn't very typical, is it?"

Lina shrugged, then shook her head. "No. I've never had this happen before. It's weird." She looked out the window at the Orpheum theatre.

"Sure, I get that. But what we do at the clinic has, you know, a philosophy around it, in a way, and these are sort of interesting times with the stigmatization of mental illness, for instance this viral Facebook post and everything." Annick stopped and drank from her coffee, angry at herself for having come so close to the topic so early on. She was sure that she could see Lina raising a perfect, tattooed eyebrow. "Are you sure I can't get you anything to drink?"

"I said I was fine."

"Do you know anything about cognitive behavioural therapy? How it works?"

"No."

Annick waited for her to elaborate, but she didn't. "No?"

"*No*," Lina said, no longer hiding her hostility. "I don't know how they make an Orange Julius, either, but I did a bus ad and it was fine."

"I'm sorry, did I do something to offend you, Lina?"

Lina shook her head, letting out a long breath. "No. Sorry. I don't know what caustic behavioural therapy is, but I don't think it will be a problem."

"Cognitive. CBT, for short. Cognitive behavioural therapy." Annick found herself babbling, trying to rein herself back in.

"Okay," said Lina, shrugging very slightly.

"Um, we use CBT to treat a wide range of anxiety issues and mental health–related problems. Do you have any experience with anything like that?"

"No."

"Or—grief? Death of a loved one, someone close to you?"

"When is the shoot? Mr. Blair said it was for a pamphlet? Is this, like, religious?"

"Mr. Blair?"

"My boss? He owns Agar, the agency?"

Annick decided to lay one of her cards down. "He owns Babylon Rivers, too, doesn't he?"

"Uhh—okay?" Lina said, growing visibly more suspicious. "What does that have to do with anything?"

"No, nothing, sorry—"

"Where I work and what I do are my business. You hiring me for a shoot doesn't mean you own me. You don't get a say in how I make my living."

"Absolutely not, absolutely not. You're right." What was it about this girl that flustered her so that she was flailing like this? "Please, that wasn't my intention. I just—it's just that I read about that young man, who got killed, and... he worked there too, didn't he? At the club?"

"This is so fucked up. I'm leaving."

"You worked with Jason, the young man who was killed, didn't you?" Annick wasn't so much laying cards onto the table anymore as she was watching them shoot out of her hands after a faulty shuffle.

Lina shot up from her seat. "What the *fuck* is your problem, bitch?"

"Easy. Sit down. Please. Please sit down."

"Why should I? Who the fuck even are you?"

"Can we just—I knew Jason, alright? He went to school with my brother."

"Yeah? Which fucking school?"

Annick slammed into the brick wall separating the detectives from the cognitive behavioural therapists. She didn't suppose there was much chance that Jason MacGregor had attended l'École du Carrefour, which she'd been bussed

140

to every morning in Dartmouth, Nova Scotia. *Why the fuck,* she asked herself, *aren't I better at this?*

"They went to... Lord—"

"Bullshit."

"Listen, I just want to talk to you about Jason."

Lina leaned over, her face an exquisite rendering of rage and menace, gritting teeth that looked as big as dominoes just inches from Annick's face.

"If you ever come near me again, Lewis Blair is going to snap your fucking neck." She turned and stormed from the table, her long legs making impossibly quick work of the exit, which didn't stop the men at their laptops from snatching at one last look.

Annick tried to sip from her cup, but it was empty. She looked around the café, trying to determine how many people had heard their exchange, but life had gone placidly back to normal indifference when the model had left the Starbucks.

She stared at the table, and against all odds, Annick had the start of a small, knowing smile. Though grief was intensely variable, playing out differently in every human carrier, sounding every time with the irreproducible idiosyncrasies of notes bent by the particular warp of a hand-carved wooden flute, Lina had not *presented*, to use the clinical term, as though she were simply in mourning. There was something complicating her grief. She had arrived steeped in surliness and irritation, but this wasn't the typical boredom and malaise of a beautiful person exhausted by regular-looking people taking up their time. There was something else at work.

No longer trying not to smile, Annick stood and approached the counter once more, buying herself a second flat white, this time to be taken to go, in a branded, reusable travel mug. Today was a day for making things right.

17

THERE WAS A special alchemy which combined fear, optimism, determination and dread into insomnia, and on the nights when that particular psychic gumbo wreaked its attendant sleeplessness, Annick could also feel the effects of the day's seven or eight coffees. Normally, ten hours of work and a liberal approach to both human sexuality and drowsy antihistamines were enough to neutralize the caffeine, but when alloyed with anxiety the coffees reared back up, frothing angry and empowered, shaking her from even the possibility of sleep. At quarter past three, Annick watched Philip's taut chest and stomach rising and falling under the thrum of his consistent snoring, and felt the irrational resentment that the exhausted always feel towards the sleeping.

If patients ever complained of sleeplessness, Annick was a consummately professional doctor, advising them in line with all of the latest research and recommended medical advice: leave the bed if you haven't fallen asleep within ten minutes, or whatever feels like ten minutes, and do something else for a little while; above all, stay away from screens.

But Annick, the temporarily insomniac private citizen, who didn't owe anybody an explanation for anything, turned over on her side and filled her face with the nauseous blue-green glow of her phone.

Back East—which was the phrase used on the West Coast to describe the middle part of the country—it was already quarter past six; stockbrokers in Toronto and sculptors in Montréal were reading the national newspapers, and now Annick, too, thumbed through the slim offerings on the cheapskate's side of the paywall.

While local coverage, labour reporting or book reviews could never be found for free, the stentorian, sententious columns of Andrew Murphy, the country's pundit laureate, were the birthright of every Canadian, and had more or less to be actively avoided in order to be missed. In a world of disorienting nuance and diversity, Murphy was the steady, droning voice of paternal, centre-right Anglo-Saxon calm. Two or three times a week, Murphy filed opinion pieces from third base, usually on the subject of how relatively easy it was to get to home plate.

IT'S NOT THAT WE'RE HEARING VOICES—IT'S THAT WE AREN'T
ANDREW MURPHY

In one of my favourite episodes of the classic sitcom *Seinfeld*, the eponymous Jerry turns to his wacky factotum Kramer to insist that a particularly absurd situation was akin to a *Twilight Zone* episode whose protagonist wakes to find a world where, though he is the same as he ever was, everyone else is transformed. When Kramer has the temerity to ask which episode that was exactly, Jerry grudgingly admits that it's a fair description of more or less every episode of the show.

If that ineffable, eerie feeling—that either the world has gone crazy, or else one has oneself—was often used as fodder for *both* of those long-running series, it's easy to see why. It's one of the most unsettling feelings that a social animal like we humans can have. Sadly, it's also nearly constant in a world like ours, where polite opinion is straitjacketed and censored, while fast-proliferating social media platforms simultaneously give vent to the ugliest fringes of our collective id.

Sorry, should I not have said "straitjacketed"? Was that unforgivably insensitive to the, er, differently mentally adjusted? If that sounds crazy (I know, I know—lock me up!), it isn't. In the decades since the movement to deinstitutionalize mental patients wreaked uniform havoc on our urban centres, turning the patently imbalanced out onto the streets to swim or, more often, sink, our national conversation has gone similarly off the rails. The official discourse has strained every hypersensitive euphemism it can possibly marshal in order to describe both behaviour, and individuals, that are just plain nuts.

And what has been the perfectly predictable fallout of these decades of sanitized speech, in which any impolitic or uncomfortable observation has been banished to the politically incorrect basements of unsanctioned thought? Well, it eventually bubbles up into the living room, but not in the way we expect it.

Is last week's viral Facebook post by bereaved Vancouver security guard Mike Collis a helpful, thoughtful contribution to the debate on mental health stigma across the country? Well, I guess it depends on your definition of helpful—or, if you prefer, what you see in the Rorschach test. Sure, it might just appear to be a formless stain. But sometimes we have to look closer.

As we have seen with regard to politics, campus speech and environmentalism, when regular people are given the freedom to voice their real, impolite opinions as opposed to officially sanctioned pieties of inclusivity, they tell different tales than we're used to hearing. Mike Collis doesn't seem to me a man given to French philosophy or postmodernism. He seems, instead, to be stricken with that disease that so often hits people who work for a living: *telling-it-like-it-is-ism*. Incapable of mustering mawkish metaphors and government-decreed solidarities to describe imbalanced outbursts, the Mike Collises of this word are letting us know—in a way that's admittedly sometimes clumsy, sometimes rude, sometimes ill-advised—what they *really* think.

And if you want to ignore that, then I think you're nuts.

Annick heaved her phone across the room and into the hamper, then chased it to make sure it hadn't broken. Spitting murmured curses, she stomped into the living room, pacing the length of the windows facing the harbour.

Once again, she was forced to reflect on the dissonances between the consummately professional Dr. Boudreau and the living, breathing Annick. As Dr. Boudreau, she had innumerable times advised patients not to make irreversible decisions at moments of high anxiety, deep depression or bubbling anger. The anxiety mind, flooded with adrenaline, was uniquely ill-equipped to plan for the long term, and she counselled patients not to quit jobs, break off relationships or sign leases when moved by these animal spirits.

But as Annick Boudreau, she could write any incensed letter to the editor in the middle of any sleepless night she fucking pleased. She took the phone she had just barely managed not to break between her thumbs, and typed.

As a practising psychologist reading Andrew Murphy's most recent column, I was struck by many of the type of impious, unofficial thoughts he seems so enthused of—for instance, how lucky he is that failure to execute a working metaphor isn't a symptom listed in the DSM-5. For what it's worth, he may be relieved to know that the description of narcissistic personality disorder (wholly absent empathy and abundant, delusional grandiosity) didn't make it into the current edition of the manual either. If he's not up on those changes, of course, it's entirely understandable, since he's really, really—can't emphasize this enough—*really* not an expert. As Murphy suggests, there will always be Mike Collises in the world, flailing from a place of hurt and relative ignorance; ironically, the mental health discourse that he disparages has a great deal to offer for explaining the expression of his particular grief. But scarier than the type of populist prejudice on display in Mr. Collis's Facebook post is the cerebral, highfalutin defence of it. Mr. Murphy lets Mr. Collis run interference for him, hiding behind his more frank language a thesaurus-checked, country club version of more or less the same thing. As worried as doctors used to be about urban legends that hand-rolled cigarettes were healthier, they were arguably more worried about sophisticates like Edward R. Murrow smoking on air and making it seem okay. Popular ignorance is one thing, but with the imprimatur of society's opinion-makers, it's a more deadly thing entirely. Oh, and I promise that's the only time anyone will compare Andrew Murphy to Edward R. Murrow.

Dr. Annick Boudreau
West Coast CBT Clinic
Vancouver, BC

Without so much as a spell-check, Annick fired the email off into the universe. She looked at the French press drying on the dish rack and tried to calculate whether she could work the coffee grinder without waking Philip. She turned on the kettle.

18

"ARE YOU OKAY? Can I make you a cup of tea?"

Lynne Herger was a tall, muscular woman at the moderate end of the tea-crusader faction of the clinic's practitioners, and Annick was too tired to wave her away. Lynne had beautiful teeth, but it had been months into her time at the clinic before Annick had realized that they were actually dentures, replacements for the teeth that had nearly dissolved from stomach acid over the long years of a debilitating eating disorder roughly concurrent with Lynne's time as a high-level ballerina.

In using cognitive behavioural therapy to treat bulimia, anorexia and binge eating, maintaining a countenance of nearly perfect non-judgment with her patients in relation to choices about food and body was foremost among Dr. Herger's tools. She had long ago mastered the perfectly neutral expression with which to ask if a patient felt better or worse after eating a tub of ice cream, and she gathered her features in the same immaculate kindness now as she took in the heavy black bags under Annick's bloodshot eyes and offered, in response, to steep a small clutch of stringy tea leaves in a cup of lukewarm water.

"Thanks, Lynne, I think I'm going to indulge in something a little harder," said Annick, still undecided as to whether than meant another multi-shot coffee in order to

148

wring a few more hours out of the day or, since she'd seen her final patient, whether it would be a throat-burning intoxicant to usher her out of half-measures and right into oblivion.

"Okay," Lynne said, pouring the water from the heated tap on the cooler into a cup containing a metal ball full of dried chamomile flowers. "You just let me know if you change your mind, okay, Annick?"

"You're the best, Lynne, thank you."

Lynne stood with her mug, teasing the thin chain attached to the ball uselessly, seemingly having nothing left in the kitchen area to hold her there, but not wanting to leave. Annick grimaced against the inevitable kindness to come.

"Annick…"

"Yes, Lynne?"

"I don't—I wouldn't want you to think that I was interfering…"

Well…

"Please, Lynne. Don't worry about it."

Lynne nodded, but stood fast, and Annick realized that she wasn't sure whether "don't worry about it" had been an admonishment not to pry, or an invitation to ask away. Wishing she was assertive or sociopathic enough to let it be the former, Annick offered an exhausted assurance that it was the latter.

"I mean don't worry about sticking your nose in. Shit—you know what I mean. Feel free to ask your question."

"Are you… okay, lately? I mean—like lately, over the past week or so?"

"I—why do you ask?"

Lynne sat down in the seat next to Annick, turning towards her chair.

"It's nothing at all that you've done wrong. You've been the same pleasure to be around, and everything's fine with the communal spaces—I just, I'm not sure. I've had the sense over the past few days that something is troubling you. And then today, you just look so tired—"

"Uh oh."

"No, you know what I mean. And you said so yourself, at lunch. I guess I was just wondering if there was anything I could do?"

Annick laid her hand on Lynne's wrist, shuffled it back and forth gently, then squeezed softly.

"Not for nothing are you a psychologist, my friend," Annick said, and Lynne shrugged and smiled self-effacingly. "I can't get into the details, because it's about a patient—but a patient of mine is in very serious trouble, and I've been taking it home with me."

"I should have known. I should have known that it would be a patient. Trust *you* to eat yourself up over patient."

"It's always about eating disorders with you, isn't it?"

It took a few seconds before Lynne pursed her lips conspiratorially and slapped Annick gently on the leg. "Stop it!"

"I've been trying to help this patient, and I'm not even sure if I can. If maybe I'm making things worse."

Lynne frowned. "What kind of trouble is it?"

"I'm not sure I should say. But it's extracurricular. Non-clinical. Or at least—well, strictly speaking, it's non-clinical."

"Annick, you can't fix every corner of their lives."

"No, it's not like that, exactly." In the fog of her exhaustion, Annick tried and failed to find the right words. "I feel a responsibility. I feel like—part of what he's... they're going through has been exacerbated by the treatment that I've been giving."

"I don't understand."

Annick shook her head. "No, I said that wrong. Lynne, I'm sorry, I'm too tired to put my words together in the right order."

"I get it."

"I just, I feel like I have to help them."

Lynne took a contemplative draw from her mug, the tea still only a weak yellow. "You know that I don't specialize in OCD. But the questionnaires you hand out, at the beginning of a course of therapy?"

"Yes?"

"They always ask about whether the potential patient feels unduly responsible for bad outcomes—even when their only power over them is entirely imaginary."

"That's right. The feeling of omnipotence, that only carrying out a ritual compulsion can prevent terrible things from happening."

"And if they don't prevent them?"

"To them, it's just as bad as if they'd purposely caused the harm."

"What I'm saying is, the belief that you both can and have to prevent all the world's dangers—"

"Is crazy."

"Well, I wouldn't put it like that."

They sat for a few moments in silence except for Lynne's sipping. Then she asked, "Oh—how are things going with the new pamphlets?"

~

As Annick pressed out of the front doors of the office building, onto the block perpendicular to Cambie with its mix of heritage residences and medical agencies, she checked her phone for messages even though she knew she hadn't heard any notifications. It was nearly seven and the traffic had already started to slow down, the metered parking emptying along the block. Annick took only a second to ask herself why the large black SUV across the street was idling its engine before she turned towards the main artery two blocks away.

As she walked, the vehicle pulled slowly out of its space and crawled, at first just behind her, then alongside her. She looked up to see who was driving it, but the tinted windows were closed and opaque, and it wasn't until she'd gone nearly half a block that she realized that the driver was openly shadowing her. She stopped for a second, and the SUV stopped with her.

"Can I help you with something?"

The motor hummed in response, the windows staring like a pair of sunglasses.

"What? What is it?" she yelled again, with more confrontation in her voice. Her mind pitched back to Halifax, to Gottingen Street, to bush parties and house parties where the girls, not far behind the boys, had preened and projected toughness. "What's your fucking problem?" She felt the lips curling up over her teeth, baring more of her seething anger the longer the truck sat stupidly there.

Annick looked up and down the block, seeing no one on the side street with her, the closest people still a block and a half east, on Cambie Street. She stared back at the windows of the truck.

"Did she send you?" she hollered. "Is that what this is?"

She started walking again, a little faster but careful not to seem like she was running, and this time the SUV stayed parked where it was.

She turned to check that the street she was about to cross was clear when the tires of the SUV screamed in exertion, hurling the vehicle along the distance that she'd put between them, then jerking left onto the small street before Cambie, screeching to a stop right in front of her, blocking the way.

"You fucking asshole!" Annick yelled, extending a middle finger, then realizing that it was shaking. She stepped to the left in order to get around in front of the suv, but it lurched forward; she walked a few steps to the right and it whirred in reverse.

Annick tried to maintain her stare into the driver's inscrutable window, tried to camouflage her trembling. They stood for something close to a minute. The body and mind that had been so tired as she left the office were now alive with adrenaline and panic, every sound amplified, her pupils opening to let in more of the summer's evening light. She felt the sweat break out between her shoulder blades and run down her back. She felt each in the litany of symptoms she explained to patients suffering from panic attacks; she explained the misfiring software of anxiety, the fight-or-flight instincts in the body firing up for what it thought was survival but was usually just a work meeting or a job interview or a date or a fleeting memory of the night a parent had died.

This time, though, it wasn't misfiring. This really was fight or flight. And she didn't know which to choose.

The tires squealed again and the suv bolted away down the block, taking a hard and screeching right, roaring audibly for what must have been twenty seconds after it was no longer visible.

Annick wanted more than anything to sit on the curb, but she was afraid that they might come back. Instead she ran for the crowds on Cambie as though they were air just on the other side of the water's surface. She was nearly vibrating as she joined the flow of humanity, hearing everyone's conversations and seeing everyone's faces but not able to make sense of any of them, dropping her wallet at the toll gates to the SkyTrain station as she fumbled with her fare card. She felt like she had to move until the very second that she sat down, at which point she knew she wouldn't be able to—she avoided the escalator and trembled along the metal railings on the way down the stairs. She paced the platform until the SkyTrain arrived, pushing rudely past the people trying to get out, negotiating their luggage from the airport. She took a seat next to a window, but when a man sat down next to her she leapt up again, fairly scurrying along the aisle until she saw an old woman, sitting in front of two other women, and sat down next to her. She texted Philip to meet her in front of Waterfront Station, so that she wouldn't have to walk home alone.

For now, at least, it would be flight.

19

"CAN I TALK to you for a second?"

Cedric was waiting at the threshold to his own office wearing a long, weary face.

Annick was emerging from a second consecutive sleepless night, only this time she was also chaperoned to work by Philip as though she were his daughter rather than his girlfriend, shepherded up the elevator and right into the reception area of the clinic. She could feel the adolescent sullenness on her own features, her jaw set in a determination not to be fucked with, a resentment both at being treated as though she were somehow not safe and her simultaneous awareness of the fact that she probably wasn't. The travel mug was, thus far, the week's only success story, having made it through several days of service now, but at this point it was empty, and hung limply from her fingers, dangling with Damocletian possibility. Despite their being peers, she felt like an ill-disciplined student entering the principal's office as she followed Cedric and shut his door.

Still standing, Cedric picked up a newspaper that had been lying on his desk and opened it to the Letters page.

"Can we talk about this?"

Through the insomniac fog, it took a full three seconds for Annick to remember that she had written a letter to the editor in response to Andrew Murphy's obnoxious column—a letter that, given the concentration of major media ownership in Canada, was probably running in as many newspapers as carried Murphy's thrice-weekly pontifications. Annick raised her shoulders in deflection.

"What is there to talk about?"

"Annick, you shouldn't need for me to tell you that this isn't okay."

"You are absolutely right—I don't need you to tell me that it isn't okay."

"Can we start this again?"

"Why?"

"Because this doesn't feel, to me, like a dynamic conducive to a helpful conversation."

"Spare me your fucking sanctimony, Cedric, alright?"

"Okay, let's talk about this later. You're clearly not in any position right now to—"

"No, Cedric, let's talk. You wanted to talk about it right now, you're the one who was lurking in wait as I arrived—"

"That is absolutely unfair—"

"I don't know how many times you'll need me to remind you of this over the course of our professional lives, but I sure as shit hope it's a shrinking number—you are not my boss, Cedric. You are not my superior. We are colleagues, we are equity partners in a practice—"

"Yes, goddamn it, equity partners in a clinic whose bloody name you signed to this juvenile, guttersnipe letter! Equity partners in a goddamned clinic whose good name has been marshalled for puffery and egotistic conflict in the pages of a major newspaper chain. Tell me again, Dr. Boudreau, how I have no right to be angry?"

Annick bobbed her head, shook the heel of her right foot, as she tried to think of an angle from which Cedric was incorrect. The walking embodiment of calm and equanimity made sinewy flesh, a "goddamn" from Cedric exploded with the conversational force of a string of *motherfuckers* from anyone else. She looked into the corner of the room, avoiding his steady gaze through square glasses, his stern but open face, and shook her head.

"I'm sorry. I shouldn't have written the letter. Or else I shouldn't have signed the name of the clinic."

"And so why did you?"

"Doesn't it ever bother you, the flattening out of everyone's opinions? I wanted to give the name of the clinic so that, I mean Jesus—so that people would know that for once, for one time, they were hearing from someone who knew what they were talking about."

"Annick, I didn't disagree with a word in the letter. It was smart, it was sharp. Hell, girl, it was funny."

"Oh, sure—and since when do you have a sense of humour?"

"Easy now. Just because a wine is dry doesn't mean you can't taste it."

Annick rolled her red eyes.

"But there are norms of both etiquette as well as ethics which have been compromised by your having written it," he continued. "We're not clergy, but our patients nevertheless approach us expecting a certain dignity, a removal from the fray. We don't roll in mud, Annick."

Annick nodded bitterly.

"And ethically," Cedric said, waving his hand in something like a conjuring gesture. "Ethically, in my opinion, this letter places the confidentiality of your patient at risk."

Annick was dumbfounded. "Excuse me?"

"He is your patient, isn't he?"

Annick bluffed for time. "Who?"

"The young man, being held for murder. Sanjay Desai. I've seen the fellow in the waiting area, seen him paying for sessions at reception. And I think that if someone were to see you coming out swinging in such force for him, they could fairly easily deduce that—"

"No, sorry, Cedric. I'll go with you on the norms of bullshit etiquette, fine, of dirtying myself in the fray. But nobody else reading that letter has seen Sanjay in this office, seen him paying up front. Anybody reading that letter would see a doctor taking perfectly understandable, whatever, *umbrage* at a loud-mouthed, Southern Ontario Cicero flapping his gums about something he knows sweet dick all about, and that she's given her professional life over to."

"That may be."

"No, it is."

"Fine."

"I won't write any more letters. Alright? Or if I do, I'll write them as an individual. But the Ph.D. is mine, for the record. It's my goddamn doctorate I'm signing next to my name."

"No one ever said anything different..."

"No Cedric, you just implied it. Brought me in here like I don't know my responsibilities to this clinic, to my patients—"

"Are you involving yourself in the legal difficulties of this young man?"

"Excuse me?"

"I think my question was quite clear, Dr. Boudreau."

"Don't you 'Dr. Boudreau' me, you pompous—"

There was a timid knock at the door to Cedric's office, and suddenly Annick wondered how loudly they had been talking. All of her self-possession, her whole sense of calibration, had been worn down by the waking hours she'd spent over the past two nights.

"Yes?" Cedric asked of the door.

It opened slightly and Marcel, the delicately constructed receptionist who wore a thin, long-sleeved sweater even in these summer months, and who looked at them through tentative eyes that seemed like fragile glass bowls, leaned the large head at the end of his thin neck just past the threshold.

"I'm sorry to interrupt."

"It's fine," the doctors said in unison.

"Dr. Boudreau, there's someone here to see you."

"Really? Who? I don't have any sessions until ten today."

"It's a Mr. Blair."

~

Lewis Blair leaned over the framed degree on the wall of Annick Boudreau's office and made a face like the very idea of a school was funny. When she'd found him standing at reception, Blair had taken in her chest and her hips before meeting her at the eyes, his overly manicured silver beard framing the kind of smile that sent fingers reaching into purses for bear spray. Blair was tall, taller than Cedric, and wore a denim shirt with pearl snap buttons, untucked over a pair of tight black corduroy pants and blue leather tennis shoes that weren't meant for tennis. He'd held a hand heavy with jewelry out for her to shake, and had taken the opportunity to inspect her chest again as he did.

"McGill University, huh?" He said stupidly, and just as stupidly, Annick answered:

"Yup."

Lewis Blair turned, smiling. He jerked a thumb westward. "I went to Sauder," he said, then added by way of clarification, "business school here at UBC."

"I know it, yes."

"Boudreau, Montréal—you a Frenchie?" Blair had given the question a bouncy jocularity meant to dull the bigotry, but Annick didn't roll with it.

"I'm an Acadian."

"Ah, Cajun! The real East Coast. Still, the accent's cute as hell. One summer about a million years ago I worked in Ottawa and we used to go over to Hull on the weekends to drink and meet the French girls, learn about, oh, the solitudes..."

"Gatineau."

"Sorry?"

"It's called Gatineau now."

"Is it? Well, I haven't been in a while. I guess everything's Frenched-up out that way these days, isn't it?"

"You know, I've always thought it was so unfair."

"What's unfair?"

"Like you say—we sound so cute when we speak English. But you guys just sound stupid when you speak French."

"Well, I don't speak a word of the stuff. I just know that these little girls, the little girls in Hull? When those little girls said '*Oui*,' we said 'Wheeeeeee!'"

Blair sat in the patient's chair, and Annick wished that her desk wasn't up against the wall, that she could get it between the two of them, but instead she sat closer to him than she would strictly have wanted to.

"Miss Boudreau—"

"Dr. Boudreau."

"Well that's right, isn't it? Why, we were just talking about that, weren't we?" he said, pointing at her diploma. "Where's my head?"

"We don't find heads here, Mr. Blair, we just help clear them out."

Blair let out a thunderclap of what sounded like genuine laughter. "That's good. You've been waiting to use that one, haven't you?"

"What can I help you with, Mr. Blair? I have a patient coming in twenty-five minutes."

"Oh, well, I'm not going to snatch nearly that much from you, missy. I'm here because I'd like to make a donation, for the good work that you people do here."

"Sorry?"

"I'm not going to beat around the bush—"

"Why would you? This isn't Gatineau."

Another explosive laugh. "Goddamn, sweet pea! You go right for the throat."

"Why don't you just state your business."

Blair dropped his face in a pantomime of hurt and consternation.

"I read your little letter today, in the newspaper, Miss Boudreau. And I hope you won't respond here in a way that's prejudicial, but, well—little Mikey, Mike Collis? That's my nephew."

"And an employee, no? Doesn't he work at your club?"

"Sure, I like to help my family. We don't let him onstage though, the little retard has two left feet."

"I've never much liked that word."

"What, 'little'? Me neither. But I think we might have that in common," Blair said, running his eyes now very deliberately over Annick's softer parts. "But of course just because someone is family, that doesn't mean we see eye to eye on everything. I mean, hell, sometimes it can mean just the opposite. And though I love my sister's son like he were my own, I don't mind telling you that I was ashamed of what he wrote about that boy. The murderer."

"Alleged."

"Sure," Blair said, smiling. "Anyhow, I wanted to, as it were, balance out my family's karma in these things, and make a donation to your little clinic here, show you that the Blair family isn't all as insensitive as our young, dumb ones. So I was thinking I'd like to write a cheque, just for a little something, say ten thousand dollars, to do our part. And I'd want you to think of it not just as coming from me, but from all my employees."

"Well, that's incredibly generous of you, Mr. Blair—"

"It's just the way God made me."

"—but we're not set up to accept donations."

"Well, you know, I figured you might say that, and so I figured I could just make the cheque out to you personally, and you yourself could just sort out the best way to put it to work for mental health."

"No. Thank you."

Blair stared at her for a second, let a switch get thrown inside his head behind a wry and angry smile, and he reached out and took a handful of Annick's chocolate peppermints. He unwrapped them slowly, letting the foil drop to the ground. As he chewed, he giggled as though along with her, reaching a finger back into his mouth to dislodge the sticky bits from his teeth. His right index finger was covered in waxy, melted chocolate.

"That's not the kind of operation you run, huh? You don't take money from outsiders?"

"No, it's not the kind of operation we run."

"Just what kind of fucking operation do you run, sister? Because I tell you what, I've got a little girl who works for me—"

"Keep saying 'little girl,' Mr. Blair. See if this time, I clutch my pearls. See if this time, my skin crawls right across the room."

Blair smiled like a shark. "There's a little girl who works for me, a little Oriental girl, pretty as a Ming vase. Probably just as easy to break, too. And she says there's some chubby little thing been pecking at her, bothering her. *Harassing* her. Setting up fake photo shoots just to talk to her."

Annick smiled and shrugged her shoulders.

"So when she tells me this, the little girl in my care, I have to ask myself if she's being hounded by some dyke slob who wants to get her snout wet, or else some bloodhound bitch who thinks she's sniffing a trail for Sherlock Holmes?"

"Get out of my office, Mr. Blair. You tell Lina Peng not to flatter herself, and you tell the asshole with the SUV to find another block to park on."

Blair smiled again and ran his finger along the inside of his mouth one more time, picking out another large piece of half-chewed chocolate mint. He dropped another wrapper on the floor.

"Just so as you know, Lina's not going to help you with anything. And you come back into her orbit in any way, little comet, you're going to crash right into Jupiter." Blair stood, looking at the last chocolate in his hand, still in the wrapper, before tossing it back into the jar. He pointed at the candies. "You know I'm just jealous as all hell of those little fucking chocolates? They go straight to that ass of yours."

He smiled again, nodding his head, and turned back towards the diploma on his way out. He tapped the glass with his wet finger, smearing it.

"Well what do you know? You were right, missy—it says it right here. *P-H-D.*"

20

"NONE OF THIS—NONE of this is good. This is... this is all very, very bad."

They were Philip's first words in several minutes, as he and Annick rounded one corner of the harbour, taking the seawall now past the Rowing Club, near the statue of Lord Stanley himself, of annual hockey championship fame, desecrated by the birds of his eponymous park as much as any symbol of the British Empire at the hands of Mau Maus or Irish Republicans. The lights of the boats and the marine Chevron station marked out the dimensions of the water that was now nearly the same shade as the mountains and the sky. They had been walking much slower than usual, as Annick went over the sickening details of her encounter with Lewis Blair; recounted, again, the terrifying episode with the black suv; and admitted for the first time to the abortive attempt at smoking out Lina Peng.

Philip breathed through his nose, as he always did whenever he wasn't sleeping. At night, the sides of his mouth lolled open sideways, emitting the erratic pulse of something close to sleep apnea, a contrast of literally breath-taking irony to the controlled, centred calm of his waking hours. Though he kept a calm in his face and in his voice, Annick could tell that he was angrier, more frustrated and more terrified than she had ever seen him.

"Please, Phil."

"Please what?"

"Please don't be silly."

"Silly."

"I'm sorry, I don't mean—"

"I never asked you to tell me anything that you couldn't tell me about this. Never asked you to tell me anything about the patient, your patient."

"No. You didn't."

"Now you come to me and you tell me you know who really killed the kid—"

"I never said that. I said I was pretty sure. I had—I have an idea. I had a theory that seemed to me to be plausible, that felt like a place to start, and so far every sign I've come across since then indicates that I was right."

"So you sit down with this woman, your *suspect*," Philip was hissing, trying to get across his anger and keep a lid on his volume. "She stands up the second you mention her dead boyfriend and threatens to sic one of the most connected guys in the city on you, and I'm supposed to say what, Annick? What do you want for me to say?"

"I don't know. You aren't responsible for fixing every problem in front of me, Philip."

"Bullshit, Annick. Not just bullshit, but hypocrisy. Holy fuck, physician heal *thyself*. How in the hell did we ever get to a place where you were poking around a murder to start with?"

Annick stared out at the water, seething. A ways off, a massive cruise ship towered up against the walkway flanking the convention centre, and the din of the partying was just outside the bounds of the audible, but just within the realm of the imaginable.

"I feel so goddamn helpless because, I don't know. Jesus.

You're in *trouble*. You are in trouble, Annick, with serious, heavy people. This girl Lina, she's got weight behind her."

"So you don't think I can get it from her?"

"Hold on, what? What do you mean?"

"You don't think I can get her to admit to killing him? To admit that it was in self-defence?"

Philip took a dazed beat before responding. "Annick, are you serious? You think I'm worried about whether or not you'll get a confession? We need to neutralize a threat to your safety. We're talking about harm reduction, here, not *winning*."

"And where does that leave him?"

"Who, Blair?"

"Sanjay. The kid, the kid in jail."

"Annick—"

"The kid who's about to lose his life over something he didn't do?"

"Annick, I love you. *You*. You, the one person, the one person in a city of two million people. It's a bitch, but from everything you're telling me, both the cops and the robbers have their guy. The most convenient guy to pin all this on is already sitting in a pre-trial centre. That's the end of the line. It's not fair, but it is what it is. I feel fucking horrible for this kid if he didn't do it."

"If?"

"Yeah, if. If, Annick. *If* he didn't do it." Philip was angry again, instantly. "You remember that all this, all this danger and these threats, this is all because you had a hunch that he didn't do it, right? You, the same person who's always going on about the dangers of equating professional expertise with amateur intuition?"

"I'm not a goddamned amateur, you fucking—you asshole!" Annick was spitting enraged, thrusting an index finger at Philip, whose eyes shot through with the fear of someone whose private argument is about to become public. Philip scanned the seawall for eavesdroppers and put out his hand in a belated bid for calm.

"Easy, okay?"

"Amateur? Fuck *you*, man. You think I got that Ph.D. on a dare? For a hobby? Put together some *maudit* knitting needle money and tampon cash?"

"That's not fair. Annick, that's not fair."

"They abhor violence, Philip."

"Who? Who abhors violence? Why else did they send a guy to—"

"Not the gangsters. Primary obsessives. Patients with repetitive, intrusive thoughts don't act out the violence that terrifies them."

"Okay."

"No, Philip. It's not okay. I'm not an amateur. And I loved you because you were a scientist."

"Annick!" Philip yelled out in the voice of a person who still doesn't want to scream. Early in their relationship, each of them had had to negotiate the large gulf between the expressive Latin passions of her francophone upbringing and the cooler, more reserved tones of his Chinese one. Even now, as the love of his life was storming off along the seawall, he didn't seem able to bring himself to screech.

The cool air came off the water and failed spectacularly to share its calm with Annick. The nine o'clock gun, the blank nightly cannon blast that rang out across the Vancouver waves, sounded its short thunderclap as Annick rounded the corner near the Bayshore Hotel, and her phone buzzed with her mother's cellphone number.

"Maman," she said with alarm, as a German family in the midst of sharing a laugh pushed past her on bicycles. "It's one in the morning. What are you doing up?"

"Annick?" In her mother's mouth, her name was clogged with tears, rendered as a lamentation. "Oh, *bébé. Mon bébé...*"

"*Qu'est-ce qu'il y a*, Maman? What's going on? Why are you phoning at one in the morning? Where are you?"

"Victoria General," said Thérèse, and immediately, from her perch watching the North Shore mountains, Annick's mind went to the red-brown brick building at the southern end of Halifax, on the other side of the country and out of what seemed like a completely different time; a hospital in such a sagging and advanced state of decay that its patients had to brush their teeth with bottled water and take sponge baths instead of showers in order to avoid the legionnaires' disease in the pipes. She shuddered, and took her heart up into her throat.

"What happened, Maman?"

"*Il est tombé dans les pommes*," Thérèse cried, and then wept into the phone.

"Mom," Annick shouted, hoping to sober her mother with the discordant English. "Who did? Who fainted? Dad?"

"*Oui.*"

"Did you take him to emergency?"

"We've been here for hours."

"Are you going home now?"

"*Non.*"

Annick felt a bile rise up out of her empty stomach, carrying with it the acid of every coffee she'd had since morning, and she spat it over the railing and into the seawater.

"*Pourquoi?*"

"You were right. You were right, *mon coeur.*"

"Cancer?"

"Colon cancer. They have him now, they are doing emergency surgery, *demain matin.*"

"I can be there for tomorrow morning, Maman. Just let me—"

"*Non! Non*, it's too much at once."

"Don't be insane. I am coming to Halifax."

"*J'ai dit non*," her mother yelled, and Annick reared back. "*C'est trop*. We have too much in our hands and Roméo doesn't want you to see him in this way."

"You're joking? You're fucking joking?"

"*S'il te plaît*, Annick. Stay home for now, okay? Okay, *ma chouette*? I will need you when we go back home. After, without the help from nurse and doctor. He will recover and then, they don't know, maybe he needs chemotherapy *après*."

"*Mère de Dieu...*"

"I know, *chérie*."

"What did they say? Did they say what stage? What his chances are?"

"They just said we came in later than we should."

"Assholes."

"*Non, bébé*. One asshole."

"Who?"

The tears had nearly gone out of her voice. "Don't make me say it while he's in surgery."

"Call me as soon as he's out of the operating room, *d'accord*?"

"*Oui, chouette*."

"Can you go home and get some sleep tonight?"

Thérèse laughed softly. "Is Philip with you?"

"No," said Annick, looking up in the direction from which she'd come, and seeing Philip moving at a lazy stride. "Sorry, yes. I was wrong. He's here."

"Give him love from us?" Thérèse said, the returning tears twisting a question out of a definitive statement.

"*Je t'aime*, Maman."

"Je t'aime fort, fort, ma chouette."

Annick hung up her phone and watched Philip lop-ing towards her, face full of contrition. When he came to within an arm's reach of her, he dropped his chin and raised his eyes.

"I'm sorry," he said.

Annick fell into his chest and sobbed for the second time in a week.

～

Half A Mind to Kill (1994) was eighty-seven minutes long and had an 89 percent match with Annick's viewing history, and as a domesticated Philip was now stretched across her lap like the kitten her father's allergies had always prevented her from having, roaring like the riding mower she'd never wanted, and since sleep didn't seem to be lurking anywhere in the corners of her night, she started watching.

Dimitri, played by a young Johnny Depp, was a killer unhinged by a series of unsubtly drawn Oedipal encoun-ters—told in black and white flashback sequences—who had now, in the black flowering of his young adulthood, set off on a Long Island murdering spree. After a tone-deaf and pencil-pushing doctor reveals the results of his Rorschach test—he had seen bats instead of birds, moths instead of butterflies, snakes instead of necklaces and dead children instead of sunsets—the enterprising psychopath sets out to take the eyes from his victims, so that he might see the innocence long denied to him by Mother. Brian Dennehy, shaped liked an upright Murphy bed, played McKellan, a hard-drinking, no-bullshit detective about to be forced into retirement by the creeping blindness brought on by cata-racts—though he was quick Brian Dennehy, at all times, to explain that he wasn't about to make excuses or look for special treatment.

There were three psychologists, or psychiatrists—Hollywood treated the terms like the news used "Sunni" and "Shia": aware that there was a difference between them but unsure as to what it was—who slithered into and out of the narrative of the picture, such as it was. There was the first doctor, who administered the fateful Rorschach—a *Der Stürmer* Jew torn from the least subconscious recesses of the anti-Semitic mind, but given the goyish name "Dr. Baker" for plausible deniability. There was a dumb, very dumb, pretty and whining girl, Dr. Tessa Blanche, who ladled bathetic excuses for Dimitri's actions from the bubbling pot of his desperately unhappy childhood, insisting with shrill, womanly stupidity that Dimitri was not a problem to be solved by the law but a person to be healed by feminine caring—that is, until her own husband, Peter, a veterinarian to boot, was found garrotted outside of his strip mall practice, empty craters where his chocolate lab eyes used to be, after which she shrieked for demented revenge. The final offender was an effete, pencil-necked dweeb named Dr. Schulz, who would pop in occasionally with the book learning that he'd picked up behind some ivy-choked wall while McKellan was out in the streets, knocking skulls together to keep the city safe. Schulz would deliver deeply nasal lectures to McKellan about the unscientific nature of his instincts, the irresponsible way in which he ignored the latest theories on psychological profiles—"That's fine for the lecture halls!" hurled McKellan heroically—and generally busted the hero's very ample balls until he himself was taken hostage by Dimitri, trying to scream from behind his duct tape gag until McKellan kicked in the windows, catapulting in from the fire escape to cure Dimitri's imbalance with "a new prescription—six tablets of lead." In doing so, paradoxically (or so the screenwriters must have hoped), a man losing his vision saves the eyes of a man who would not, until it was too late, *see*.

Annick couldn't remember at this point whether Rene Russo was supposed to be Brian Dennehy's daughter or his wife, but as they approached some sort of resolution to their either filial or romantic subplot in a crowded sub-way car stopped for some reason on the tracks, she began to feel her eyes closing despite her worries, and felt herself smiling despite everything as she slowly slumped onto Philip's shoulder, drifting into hypnagogia as the credits began to roll. Before the decisive moment, the second when mere sleepiness succumbed absolutely to sleep, she was wrenched back from the precipice of bliss by the pinging tone of an incoming email. She straightened herself up from Philip, his head still in her lap, and grabbed her phone from the side table, expecting to hear something from her mother. Instead, it was from Supriya:

Sanjay will see you.

****

Dr. Supriya Desai, Ph.D.
Associate Professor
Department of English
Simon Fraser University
Unceded Musqueam, Squamish, Tsleil-Waututh, and Kwikwetlem territories
she/her/hers

21

ANNICK HADN'T OWNED a car since she'd left Nova Scotia, leaning on the brilliantly reliable and intricately networked metro system during her Montréal years, and on the infuriating patchwork of late buses and train lines with arbitrary end points that made up Vancouver's public transit. When she was feeling generous, Annick remembered that Vancouver was essentially a Californian car city in worse weather, having had its biggest growth spurts in the mid to late twentieth century, in the years when single-passenger vehicle travel had been the apogee of aspirational civilization.

If you didn't have kids—with their need for life-saving rear-facing baby seats, or the booster seats that they seemed to have to sit on until a few months before they got their learner's licences—you could, as Annick did, undergird the missing or rotten planks in the city's transit infrastructure with membership in a car-sharing service. After adjusting the seat and mirrors and driving a few blocks with the windows down for a mostly pro forma cleansing of the air, Annick turned to Radio-Canada—and after a news briefing about the summer forest fires across British Columbia, and after a seventh unanswered call to her mother's cellphone, she and the airwaves settled into the cerebral comfort of piano- and saxophone-driven jazz.

Supriya Desai lived in one of the soaring new condominium towers along the edges of Brentwood Mall, a once second-rate suburban shopping centre that had become a new hub of transit and conspicuous consumption at the northern end of Burnaby. Supriya was waiting outside of the resplendent blue and grey lobby of the building, which must have been at least something of an embarrassment for a postcolonial professor of English, even one who had traded Marxism for postmodernism as a critical lens.

"Beautiful place," Annick said as Supriya got into the car.

"Oh, thank you. I've come to think of it with fairly intense regret."

"Really? Why's that?"

"We just moved in three years ago. I feel like if we'd stayed—we used to have a small townhouse by Burnaby Hospital, and I feel that if we'd stayed there, where Sanjay had such roots, he'd never have insisted on this bizarre adventure of renting a room in the city." Annick didn't say anything about the role Sanjay's violent thoughts may or may not have played in his decision to move.

"Where I grew up, nobody could wait to move out from their parents' house. I went to school in Montréal the September I turned eighteen and believe me, my parents would have much preferred to have me in someplace like Kitsilano. For a kid my age, Montréal was like Sodom and Gomorrah with French signage."

"Is that your background? *Québecoise*?"

"*Acadienne*," Annick said, smiling. "The *other* Frenchmen. If Québec was Pepsi to the Anglos' Coke, we were like the RC Cola to Québec's Pepsi."

"Is it really so stark?"

"Not really, I don't know. Sometimes, I guess. Parisians make fun of the accent they have in Québec, and then

Montréalers turn around and make fun of the accent on the East Coast."

"I'm fascinated by the history of the Acadians," Supriya said, staring out the window as Annick pulled off of the Lougheed Highway onto the Trans-Canada. "The reversed fortunes of settlerism, dislocation. This grammar of non-white Whiteness."

Annick nodded, for the most part following what Supriya was saying.

"And here we are now," said Supriya, "two women from homelands disrupted by the British Empire, embodying positions of relative class privilege, on unceded, stolen Indigenous territories..."

She really talks like this, Annick thought again, smiling, *all the time.*

"... and facing down an edifice of colonial justice constructed to imprison brown bodies. Like Sanjay's."

Without taking her eyes off the road, Annick laid a hand on Supriya's knee and squeezed. For a few seconds, Supriya didn't react, and just as Annick was about to pull back, Supriya laid her hand over top of Annick's.

"Thank you," she said.

Annick returned her hand to the wheel, and they rode in silence, and in the silence the question that Annick wanted to ask kept growing until its urgency was electric, a strong and burning current running through every part of her. She began stealing sidelong glances at Supriya, at first camouflaging them against highway sign readings, then hoping to get caught.

"Supriya..."

"The envelope you gave me."

Annick nearly jerked the car off the road.

"Yes?"

"Did you know that it wasn't sealed? Maybe you wanted me to read it?"

They drove in another silence just as long as the last.

"I don't know," Annick answered hoarsely. "I asked myself the same question, Supriya. I didn't realize it as I was handing it to you, but, I—it did occur to me, afterward, that maybe... I don't know. Maybe I wanted you to read it, to know that I could help. I felt—I don't mean this as a self-justification of any kind, but I felt *coincée*, um, pinched... cornered. I felt like two aspects of my commitment to care were being set against each other. I—I don't know."

Annick felt the redness rising in patches on her skin, her neck, face and chest, but the heat didn't distract from the fact that Supriya hadn't told her anything about what she'd done with the letter.

"Did you?" she asked, and Supriya looked out the window again. Annick's stomach clenched.

"No," Supriya said finally, and Annick allowed for a tentative confidence and optimism to creep in around the fringes.

"No?"

"No. I very much wanted to, when I saw that you had— that I had been given the choice. But my son has a sovereignty in his life, one compromised institutionally in every other corner of it. Right now he has lost even the basic, physical sovereignty over his own body, his own bodily functions. He's been caged. The animals who've imprisoned him have stolen the dignity of his privacy. I couldn't heap another theft on top of that."

Annick looked out at the road in front of her.

"But when I gave him the envelope, I told him what I thought. I recounted your reaction to his letter, the urgency of your bearing in response. I told him that I could tell that you were a good doctor and that I trusted you, and that I believed that he should trust you too. And I told him that if a good and decent and talented person like you were taking so active an interest in his liberation, that he had to know that he, too, was *good*."

Supriya took Annick's right hand again, clutched it firmly between both of hers.

"My son told me about his thoughts. The violence against me. He told me that he'd been worried that he was a monster, worried to tell me lest I thought so, too. And I thought of the moments when he was just a small thing, three years old, four years old, and he would scream in the night from a bad dream. Some parents will tell you that there is nothing so difficult as watching one's child in fevered sickness, to feel the overwhelming desire to trade one's own place for theirs. To *take* the sickness. But I would feel that desire most acutely when he woke screaming. That was when I felt most powerless, because I knew that I would lay my life down to save him from anything that ever threatened him from the outside. But I couldn't dream his dreams for him."

~

The Surrey Pretrial Services Centre looked like what it was: a large, mid-aughts public works commission whipped up by a right-wing provincial government running competitively in several surrounding electoral districts. The architectural style was Kafka-Ikea, and the counsel for the defence, Terry Chu, was waiting for the two of them next to a concrete flowerbed where no one had thought to plant anything.

The lawyer had a thin moustache, kept short, and the rest of his hair was long and pulled back in a loose ponytail. Even behind sunglasses, he winced into the sun, bouncing his head in welcome instead of waving his hand.

"Dr. Desai," Chu said, nodding at Supriya, then thrusting a hand out to Annick. "Dr. Boudreau. I'm Terry, I'm Sanjay's lawyer."

"I'm really glad to finally be here," Annick said, with measured frustration. Terry Chu smiled under his thin moustache.

"Our jobs are very similar in some ways, Dr. Boudreau. We both have ethical obligations to Sanjay. There was no way that I could bring you in without compromising Sanjay's privacy and without potentially compromising the case. If it did turn out that your notes, your opinion, if subpoenaed—if all that was in Sanjay's favour, then it would have been better for you to have been brought in by the other team. We coulda made them look bad that way, not only neutralized your notes but made them work for us."

"I understand that."

"You'll be able to meet with Sanjay one on one, but so you know, once you have, the conversation is fair game. They can ask him about it, they can ask you about it, and me too—I can ask you guys about it."

"Sanjay spoke to Terry after my conversation with him," Supriya offered, letting Annick know that the seal had been broken.

"Okay."

"He told me about your course of treatment, the OCD. Is it true that the diary, the notes—is it true that was something you made him do?" asked Terry.

"Well, that's not exactly how I'd phrase it but yes, it was part of our course of therapy. We'll often ask patients to note the frequency and intensity of intrusive thoughts. And especially towards the beginning of treatment, it can help to know the content as well."

"Right, and you'll say as much in court?"

"Yes, of course."

Terry smiled again. "Good, good. Jesus. It's nice to have a bit of reason for optimism here. They won't like that his story changed, but you'd say it was natural, eh, given stigma et cetera? Mental illness?"

"Of course."

"Good, good. Well, let's go in and sit you guys down together. I think he's very excited to see you."

"Sure, can I ask, though—"

"Yeah?"

"What's going on with the investigation?"

"What investigation?"

"Into who actually killed Jason."

"Again, what investigation? As far as the VPD and Crown are concerned, they have their guy."

"What about the third person's blood?"

"Oh, you know about that?"

"I told her," said Supriya.

"Right now that blood is both the carrot and the stick. When they want to soften him up, that's the blood of an accomplice that he can flip on for leniency. They figure he can admit he killed MacGregor, but if he tells them who helped him he's out sooner. But when they want to scare him, I mean scare him even more than he's already scared, they pretend they think it's a second victim, out bleeding somewhere, a loose end."

"Mr. Chu—"

"Terry, please, Dr. Boudreau."

"Terry, I think I know who actually did it."

"Annick!" Supriya shouted, eyes widened in betrayed shock. "Why didn't you tell me?"

"Because—" Annick started, before Terry took her by the crook of the arm and marched the three of them out into the parking lot.

"What do you mean you think you know who did it," he asked now, more seriously than he'd been speaking since their arrival. Supriya crossed her arms.

"The reason I haven't said anything, to you, either, Supriya, is that I don't know for sure. I'm trying to get it sorted out. The kid, Jason, he had a girlfriend. A model and dancer, maybe more, at Babylon Rivers, the club where Jason worked. Where his friend Mike still works. They had a very up and down relationship, lots of fighting, Mike even denied that they were together. And when I confronted her about it—"

"Jesus Christ..." said Terry, and held his forehead in his hand. Without taking his sunglasses off, he slipped his knobby fingers up behind the lenses and rubbed his eyes.

"She acted incredibly suspiciously, and then I started getting threats."

"Annick," said Supriya, quietly and with frustrated empathy.

"Get the fuck out of here," said Terry.

"No, it's true."

"No, I mean get the fuck out of here," Terry said angrily, pointing at her car. "Get the fuck back into your vehicle and get as far away from this case as possible while I try to figure out what to do with this."

"Do with what?"

"Is it even humanly possible that you're this stupid?"

"Listen, I don't have to—"

"Knowing full well that you could be called as a witness in this trial, you went out and poisoned your testimony with some Nancy Drew bullshit harassment campaign against the dead kid's stripper fucking girlfriend? Do you realize that you're useless to me now? Useless to Sanjay?"

"Terry, please be calm. Annick thought she was helping."

"I don't give a fuck what she thought!"

"Excuse me, you incompetent dickhead, but I had no reason whatsoever to think that I was going to be called as a witness in this trial, because you were waiting to do some Johnnie Cochran jiu-jitsu on the prosecutors, like they were going to try to get Sanjay to fit a leather glove around his serotonin. I went out, at great risk to my own personal safety, by the way, because the cops were ready to railroad my patient and his dipshit Clarence Darrow cosplay lawyer was sitting on his hands!"

The two of them seethed in Supriya's calm presence, the sun baking the asphalt underneath them.

"I'm sorry," Terry said finally. "I shouldn't have spoken to you like that."

"Okay," said Annick. "I'm sorry too."

"Terry, can we address the implications of this after Dr. Boudreau has spoken to Sanjay?"

Terry smiled hopelessly. "Dr. Desai, I wasn't speaking in, whatever, hyperbole when I said that the testimony is poisoned. I need her as far away from Sanjay right now as possible. At the very best, I mean off the top of my head, I can bring in an expert who has no relation to the case, none to Dr. Boudreau, who can comment on her session notes, talk about OCD in general. But even the session notes are tainted now. Dr. Boudreau's reliability is going to be a punching bag. You like OJ metaphors? If I'm Johnnie Cochran, you just became Mark Fuhrman."

Annick felt sick.

"But what about this sex worker woman?" Supriya asked. "What about her?"

"Can't we ask the police to look into her? At least test her blood against the third person's?"

"Based on what?" Terry said, now somewhere between hysterical and resigned. "Based on the hunch of my now-toxic witness, we'd like the police to start digging into a grieving woman's affairs? This is still a democracy, Dr. Desai."

"It's not just a hunch," Annick said lamely.

"Well, at this point," Terry said, "You'd better hope not. You'd better hope that she was mastermind enough to carry this thing off, but enough of a fuck-up to let it slip now. Because if somebody can't prove that the girlfriend did it, this woman's son is going to prison."

22

GETTING DRUNK ON white wine wouldn't have been Annick's first choice, but it was summertime, and the only bottle of red in the house had been a gift from Philip's father that they were saving for a special occasion. The deep, leathery drunk of a red wine felt better suited to the particularly melancholic version of oblivion that she was looking for, but there were three bottles of white on hand—two of them already chilled and one now sitting in the freezer—and so she made do.

She had poured the first of it into a stemless water glass, drinking it at a clip better suited to an iced tea. When Philip arrived home, he found the first bottle empty on the counter, Annick splayed on the couch and pouring from the second, with the Cyndi Lauper version of "I Drove All Night" playing on repeat from the Bluetooth speaker positioned in the middle of the glass coffee table.

"Hey," he said, putting the keys down on the granite counter of the kitchen island. "What's going on? Is it about your dad? Are we celebrating?"

"Hey, you're a science—if I lef' that bottle in the freezer and it explode?"

"Jesus Christ, Annick."

"Because how come I had a friend that kept vodka in

the freezer and—because vodka doesn't freeze and the bottle always come out so cold."

Philip poured a tall glass of water for her, cut up an orange for the electrolytes and set them in front of her on the coffee table, removing her wine glass and the second bottle after she'd pre-emptively finished it, batting his hand away. He leaned down to where she was, resting her head on the hard arm of the couch, and kissed her on the forehead. She smiled stupidly as Philip returned to the kitchen and set the kettle to boil, clicking the large blue flame to life under the water.

"Be honest, you miss my hair. The shaved it makes you feel like a lesbian."

"Actually, my wanting to have sex with you does not make me feel like a lesbian," Philip said with patience, leaning on the counter. "Given my penis and testicles and all that stuff. Not to be a gender reductionist."

"I had such beautiful long hair."

"You did. You're also beautiful now."

"It's not the men that change—they keep looking because of tits. They don't care. But I miss how little girls used to look at my hair. Like a princess."

Annick closed her eyes for a second, and Philip thought that she'd fallen asleep.

"And then I could tell 'em," she said, springing suddenly back to life, sitting up on the couch, "I could tell 'em that fuck that, I'm not a princess, I'm a psychologist. You don't have to be a stupid princess." Annick giggled, and Philip smiled with deep condescension.

"At the very least, I won't have to hold any hair back for you when you're puking later. Eat your orange, love. It'll help tomorrow."

"I fucked everything up."

The kettle whistled on the stove, and Philip removed it from the heat, pouring it into a large, handmade pottery mug that he had partially filled with lemon juice and several black tea bags. He carried it over to Annick, his face riven by confusion.

"Annick, what are you talking about?"

As he sat next to her on the couch, she nuzzled her head drunkenly between his neck and shoulder, then stood up with the sure-footedness of a baby giraffe tumbling out of the birth canal.

"Easy," said Philip. "Sit down, love."

"I fucked everything up," she said. She took the mug from Philip's hands and began sipping at it despite the heat. "I tried to help, but not in the way of I actually could."

"Stop beating yourself up, okay Annick? Let's just lie down—"

"No!" she blurted with a drunk's screeching U-turn, a tonal shift that made Philip jump back in his seat. "You were right, you said so. He needed me to be a doctor, and now I can't be his doctor to help him."

"We don't have to talk about this, Annick."

"There's nothing to talk about," she smiled. "I'm just a fuck-up. I can't help him."

"That's not on you, Annick. I don't know if you ever could have helped him."

Annick bit her bottom lip at him, and gave him another heavy-lidded smile. "You're cute, but you don't know any-thing." She giggled, put down her mug of tea and lay on the couch with her head in Philip's lap.

~

When she woke up, the apartment was dark. Philip had dis-appeared except for the sheet that he had draped over her, the couch cushion that he had placed underneath her head and the sliced oranges from earlier—half an hour ago? Two hours? Six hours?—in the evening. There was a sickly sweet tang in the back of Annick's mouth, but she felt like she could make it without throwing up, except for the buzzing, against which Annick braced the sides of her head with her fingers, until she realized that it was coming from her phone on the key table next to the front door.

The phone kept buzzing as Annick stood unsteadily, try-ing to sort whether she was still drunk or already hungover, squinting into the microwave clock to see that it was three forty-five a.m. Annick's body began to feel an apprehension about the call before her mind did, and when she picked up the phone she saw that it was, at last, her mother phoning. *Her father was dead.*

Annick felt the third set of tears in several years, or the last week, ready to start again.

"Maman?"

"*Allo, ma chouette.*"

"*Il est mort?*" Annick's sentence trembled into an upward inflection.

"*Qui?*"

"*Huh?*"

"What?"

"Papa, Maman!"

"*Non!* Why you would say even that!"

Relief and anger elbowed each other in a race to fill Annick's chest. "So why are you calling me at three forty-five a.m.?"

Thérèse tutted shamefully. "Ah, *mon Dieu. Bébé,* I'm

sorry, I complete forgot what time it is t'ere. *Fais dodo*, go back to sleep."

Annick rolled her eyes without opening them.

"How is he?"

"Who?"

"I'm going to jump off this balcony if you don't—"

"Roméo! Oh, *mon coeur*. I'm sorry I didn't call yesterday, it was so long. The doctors seem very happy with the surgery. Very soon they're gonna tell us if he needs chemotherapy."

"Really? Well, that sounds good. Or about as good as we're going to get for now."

"*T'es tu correcte, ma chère*? You sound sad."

"No, nothing, Maman. I'm sorry. It's just work. Sort of. Work-related."

"I'm so proud of you."

"Yeah, well. Don't be."

"I don't know how you do this."

"*Quoi?*"

"To see people every day in their most *tendre*, their most vulnerable position. So weak. Can you imagine your Papa, *faible*? Weak?"

Annick flipped through the deck of paternal memories: her father chopping wood, tying knots off her uncle's boat, pushing cars out of the snow, lifting four kids out of the above-ground pool, hoisting their mother up underneath a hanging sprig of mistletoe in a house shaded away by her memory, just the two of them in a halo of warm, yellow light. Thérèse began to cry, and Annick realized why she had called this early.

"*Y peut rien faire*," she sobbed.

"Of course not, Maman. Nobody can do anything after a surgery like that."

"He can't go to the toilet—"

"They went in his colon, Maman."

"Today I held his hand, tried to squeeze it. He tried to smile at me like a *bébé*, weak, weak, and he could not squeeze me back."

"I know, Maman. *Je sais*."

"What if 'e never comes back?"

"He probably won't, Maman. Not like he was."

They stayed breathing into the phone, Thérèse every now and again punctuating the comfortable silence with a small sob.

"You remember 'ow strong 'e was?"

"*Oui*."

"The day I meet him was a big party at my cousin Jean-René's, you remember Uncle JR's farm?"

"Of course," Annick smiled. "Those were always our favourite days of summer."

"JR was at the barbecue, but he had told me that he had a friend to meet me: *ton père*. We talked the whole party, we dance. Roméo played the spoon, did you ever see your father do the spoon?"

"*Oui*."

"He was so *charmant*, handsome. With his big, rough hand. I could feel it when we dance, not only in my hand but against my little back, through the shirt."

Annick thought of her father's hands. She knew the end of the story, but for the moment, she wanted to remember her father's hands.

"But JR's cousin on his other side, François, 'e was *amoureux de moi*. I never did nothing to give him no idea, but he say he have a claim on me, start yelling at Roméo. Your Papa, 'e stood, don't say nothing, 'e punch François *en pleine face*, right on the nose, the mouth, and François went right to sleep." Thérèse laughed softly. "I knew I wanted your Papa all to myself right then."

Annick raised an eyebrow. That was not the way that the violent story of their courtship at Uncle JR's farm party had ever been told. In the past tellings, the moment that Roméo threw the punch had nearly cost him everything: his imminent marriage, the as-yet-unconceived lives of his children. The young Thérèse had been appalled by the Neanderthal display of country thuggery, the sort of bumpkin violence that her own mother, Annick's Mémère Alberte, had never once tolerated in the Leblanc family home. In those past tellings, Thérèse had stormed off after the punch, asking Jean-René to leave his station at the barbecue and take her home. JR had had to plead his friend's case, and Roméo had had to swear to a life of nearly Gandhian non-violence, before the young couple could carry on with the easy flirtation of the earlier hours of the party.

Annick often had to explain the tricks of memory to her patients, people crippled by guilt from memories of grave childhood crimes that they returned to obsessively—she had to break it to them that that was not how it worked. The mind filled in the blank spots in memories with make-believe, and in time the remembrances and retellings became part of the story itself. Human memories, particularly those from childhood, were notoriously unreliable and a rotten source for developing a sense of self-worth.

But it didn't feel like Thérèse had suddenly had a clearing through which to see the memories as they had truly happened, or that she'd been spinning a false narrative all those years when relaying to the children the story of how their parents had fallen in love. It felt instead like, having watched Roméo now old and wiry, hooked up to a thousand whirring and buzzing machines and unable to shit, or piss, or squeeze her hand, Thérèse was recasting the idiotic story of his youthful barbarism as a heroic tale of rural romance.

"Maman? I should go back to bed."

"*Hunh*? Ah, *oui, oui, chouette*—I'm sorry. Go back to bed. Kiss your Philippe."

"*Je t'aime*, Maman. Don't leave me hanging like yesterday again, okay? Phone me. Please. Whatever it is, whenever it is."

"Okay. *Je t'aime, ma chère.*"

Annick tried to remember where the plug for her phone was, before finding it swimming at the bottom of her purse. She plugged the phone in to charge, and turned off the ringer, pouring herself a large glass of water that she drank too late as a balm against tomorrow's hangover. She gathered the plate of oranges from the coffee table, ferrying it to the refrigerator, taking a couple of slices for the road. As she put the peels into the compost bag she thought about her mother's story, and smiled, and then jolted.

It was too early still to tell—maybe she was still drunk, maybe she was hungover, she was certainly tired. She couldn't say whether this was inspired or pathetic, whether she'd seized upon a moment of clarity or was still in the grips of dream logic. She would think about it tomorrow. For now, she would just leave herself a note, a reminder, for when she was well-rested and functional. She grabbed the pad of paper with the magnet strip on the back from off of the fridge door, and a pen from the junk drawer.

Over her, not with her?

She took the bedsheet from the couch, dragging it behind her into the bedroom. She lay down next to Philip, kissing him on the back of the neck, feeling the vibration of his snoring on her lips, and turned to lie on her back.

She stared at the ceiling thinking for close to an hour and a half, and didn't notice when she'd passed out again.

23

"HOWEVER THIS ENDS up going, we need to remember to pitch this as a series."

"An interracial stakeout series?"

"Baby, the thing sells itself—a pair of private investigators, a sexy French-Canadian girl and a passable Chinese-Canadian man—"

"Outrageous."

"Okay, in the fictional version he can be sexy..."

"Can I remind you that I am under absolutely no obligation to be here?"

"But that's just the thing about our hero—he may be homely, and slow-moving, but he loves his woman. That's why he's always by her side, ready to help her fight crime, and then offer up his body when the case is closed."

"What's their agency called? Gotta be something French and Chinese. Go. No editing, first thing you think of."

"*Mon petit chou... Enlai.*"

"Get out of the car."

Philip reached over from the passenger seat and pinched Annick's thigh at the line of her shorts, and she slapped his hand away with a growling giggle. The summer had landed with its full weight, the new Vancouver summer of the Anthropocene, as oppressively heavy and sweat-soaked as the summers back East that a good percentage of the people in the city had moved here at least partly to get away from. Parked just outside the Tides from which Annick had watched the back door of Babylon Rivers the first time, the two of them sat in the car-share vehicle, the windows all down to little effect, and were going giddy and stir-crazy against the fear, tension and uncertainty.

A manic energy had propelled Annick through her day despite the hangover and the lack of sleep. Her sense upon waking that her reasoning had been sound, that her new reading of the situation made sense, had had the effect of a vitamin B shot, and through the impossibly long hours of work her knees had not stopped bouncing, and her fingers had not stopped tapping at her sides.

Philip was on-side now, though he'd been harder to convince earlier in the day. He'd been out for a run when Annick woke to a hangover whose power had been dulled by the electrolytic precautions she'd taken the night before. Under the hot spray of the shower, she had gone over her new theory from multiple angles, and every time she did, it fit even more tightly, made even more sense. She had heard Philip coming in as she was wrapping herself in her thick terry cloth bathrobe, her crewcut drying immediately while she explained excitedly what she'd been thinking, all wide eyes and broad hand movements, an eager and somewhat self-satisfied smile lighting up her face.

"So what you think?"

"What do I think? I mean, I guess it's plausible?"

"What do you mean, 'plausible'? Why do you have to be like that?"

"No, sorry. Look, I didn't mean to throw cold water on the idea. I just—how would you even prove it?"

"I need to talk to her again."

"But she's not going to go for that."

"That's why it needs to be a surprise. Come with me. Please?"

All day at the clinic, Annick tried to tamp down the adrenal kick that she could feel in her chest as she reflected on the night's prospects. Whether it was Cedric or Lynne or any of the others, she would avoid eye contact in the kitchenette, excusing herself from conversations before she exploded. She fought heroically to keep her full attention on the mercifully small group of patients she had scheduled to see that day, and more than once thought of calling Supriya to share her hopefulness, before deciding that that was likely premature.

Now, night had long since fallen, and if Philip's willingness to be there was flagging, he wasn't showing it, and Annick was still vibrating with energy when the back door of the club opened, and the same squat guy walked another glamorous and overly made-up young dancer down into the alleyway, seeing her into the back seat of a blue cab, then turning and jogging back up the stairway.

"She's not coming out," said Philip. "It's two in the morning. If she were going to leave, she'd have left by now. The clubs are all closing."

"Not the VIP room. Trust me, it's not covered by the same by-laws. She's in there. And she'll be coming out."

They sat for ten minutes without saying anything, Philip playing with the radio dial, listening to snippets of prerecorded talk and American classic rock. Finally he turned the radio off, and they sat in total stillness with each other, the only sounds the growing hollerings of happy drunks pouring out onto the downtown sidewalks.

"Do you know what you're going to say to her?" Philip finally asked.

"I don't, no. I mean, I don't know."

Philip nodded and looked out his window.

"I mean," Annick continued, "she's going to be scared, right? Of Lewis Blair, of what he could do to her. I just have to make it clear..."

"Make what clear?"

"I don't know.".

The door at the top of the stairs opened, a thin silhouette against the warm light of the hallway behind it. Lina turned out from the doorway and started down the stairs, and Annick was breathless.

"That's her, that's her. She's by herself!"

"Why is she by herself?"

As Annick began to answer, Lina halfway down the wooden stairs, the black SUV from outside her office pulled into the alleyway, stopping at the bottom of the steps where the taxis had.

"Shit."

"Who the fuck is that?"

"I don't know. But it's the same truck, from outside work."

The engine of the SUV still running, red tail lights glowed on the fronts of Lina's long legs as she came down the last of the stairs, and Mike Collis oozed out of the driver's door and opened the door for Lina. Grim-faced, Mike circled the back of the vehicle, lumbering back up into his seat and starting the engine.

"Shit. He's driving her."

"Annick, what do you want to do?"

Annick ran her bottom teeth over her top lip, then started the car, rolling the windows up as the air conditioning blasted with welcome alacrity from the vents.

"Annick?"

"In for a penny..."

"There's a reason they call it the sunk cost *fallacy*, baby."

Annick locked eyes with Philip before he dropped his for a moment, then brought them back up with a reluctant nod. "Alright, let's go before I have a chance to change my mind."

"*Merci, mon amour.*"

Annick waited a few seconds for the SUV, which, now that she was no longer terrified, she could see was an Audi, to travel the distance of the alleyway before she pulled across the two lanes of one-way traffic and followed it. Keeping back a good three hundred feet, she sped up when she saw the Audi turn left at the end of the block, onto another two-lane, one-way street, running in the opposite direction.

"Easy," said Philip from the passenger's seat.

The next turn was a right onto Hastings, moving east, and now Annick could rest easier, a few cars back on the artery, moving slowly through the blocks where the legal speed limit had been dropped to accommodate the sometimes dazed jaywalking of drug users who didn't have the luxury of a living room to get high in.

She followed the SUV past Chinatown, past Strathcona with its lines of millworker rowhouses transformed by magic into multi-million-dollar homes, onto the overpass above the rail lines, the large, brick, Victorian sugar refinery barely visible now behind colourful condominiums, all of them dwarfed by the dark purple mountains against the black-blue sky. As they approached Clark Drive, the Audi punched ahead, pulling forward with a roar and putting a troubling distance between the two vehicles.

"Shit," said Annick.

"We don't have a chance, it comes down to speed. You can't let him get out in the open."

The Audi got smaller up ahead, weaving between lanes.

"Just keep your eyes on him, Phil."

"I'm trying."

The howl of tires against the dry road was suddenly underwritten by a duet of screaming horns. A taxi had pulled out from the beer and wine store attached to the Waldorf hotel, making a left both too wide and too slow, blocking the Audi's route, narrowly missing its front end. Annick smiled quietly as she made up the distance.

At Commercial Drive, the Audi took a left, into the darkness of the light industrial neighbourhood at the northern end of the city's most vibrant street, long after its foot traffic fizzled to nothing besides the suspicious. The air stank from animal waste reduction, the rendering of swine flesh and industrial poultry processing, and the cars were just as thin on the ground as people.

With nothing more than a purr, the Audi gained a stunning and sudden speed again on Commercial, turning right into the intersection at Powell, past the storage facilities and artisanal coffee roasters, and Annick struggled to keep up.

"He knows we're following," said Philip.

"What an incredibly helpful observation."

"Easy now."

Annick spotted the SUV farther up Powell, roaring towards Nanaimo Street, and gunned through a controlled green made red by a waiting pedestrian.

"I'm sorry..." Annick said, unsure whether she was apologizing to the pedestrian, to Philip, to herself. The car share lunged under the weight of her foot on the gas, and they made up most of the distance between the vehicles before pulling up behind the Audi, which sat at a red, ready to explode onto the main road.

"He's going to hit the Ironworkers Memorial, take the bridge over to the North Shore," Philip said. "Once we're off the bridge, the highway is going to open right out in front of him and we won't have a chance."

"I don't think that's what's happening."

"No?"

"No, look."

The Audi stopped dead at a flashing green light. Annick didn't breathe as she watched its driver's side door swing open, followed by a thick pair of legs in tapered sweatpants, pulling a grizzly bear's upper body out behind them. Mike was lipless with predator rage, seething, and for a long and nauseous moment he just watched them.

"Fuck this, I'm getting out," said Philip.

"The hell you are," Annick said, calmly.

Mike sauntered to the front of the car, Annick's headlights illuminating him theatrically, making him appear unreal, or hyperreal; dream-like. He was reduced to an image produced by the mind, all the more terrifying but not really in front of her, not able to hurt them, really. Then his knee bent up towards his stomach, his arms spreading as though he were about to take flight, and he plunged his foot into the front of the car's hood, caving it in. Resting the sole of his shoe in the dent that he'd left, Mike rocked the vehicle for what could only have been a few seconds but felt like much longer.

"Jesus Christ," said Annick.

"He's out of his mind," said Philip.

Mike was standing, now back in a more comfortable and familiar bouncer's stance, feet wide apart, and he spat on the windshield.

"You're not gonna leave her alone, huh? You think she killed Jason? Jason was our friend, she never would've killed him."

Before entirely realizing that she had even opened the door, Annick was stepping out of the car, reflexively dodging the protective hand Philip shot out to retrieve her. Mike was clearly startled as he watched Annick rise, still standing behind her door, shielding herself, and he tried to hide his surprise with a sarcastic grimace.

"You think she killed Jason?"

"Nope. I know who killed Jason."

Mike glowered skeptically, and a fire engine's siren wailed farther up Nanaimo Street.

"Follow me," he said.

24

AS THEY PASSED the hulking darkness of the horse racing track, Mike signalled onto the last turnoff before the highway, down onto the curlicue overpass that led to the New Brighton Pool, a summer oasis of public recreation with a stunning alpine vista, encircled by the rusty clang of port-authorized transportation trucks and the railways that had been the whole reason for the city in the first place. There was no speed to the chase anymore, and now the two cars were a convoy, driving like a group of friends too big for just one vehicle.

Mike pulled the Audi into the dusty overflow parking lot, which sat empty and dark except for the summer moon and the cast-off glow of the tall halogens lighting the train tracks. Annick pulled the car share in just a few feet behind the Audi.

Philip took his seat belt off, moved to the front of his seat. Without taking his eyes off of Mike's truck, he spoke with dead calm to Annick.

"Can you make this work?"

"I have no idea."

"What does he want?"

"Don't know."

"But like, I mean—is she going to be willing to say any-thing right now?"

"I don't see how we can leave her like this," Annick said. "And I'm not sure we have much choice."

Mike's door opened more slowly this time, his steps down from the driver's seat more deliberate. He swivelled to face them, smiling, raising his hands above his head as though he were headed into a wrestling ring.

"Let's fucking do this, for real. Come on, bitch. Let's finish this."

"You get out of this car again and you are officially single, lady."

Mike slapped the front of the car in a violent burlesque of playful. "Huh? What do you say? Step out and end it?"

"Single's if I'm lucky. What I'm really worried about is you being a widower."

"Maybe we'll just go to heaven together."

"Some science reporter you turned out to be."

"Yeah that's what I thought, you fucking bitch," Mike said outside, seeing that they weren't moving and waving them off with disgust, then turning back towards the suv.

"What's this?" Philip asked.

"It's not real," said Annick, and as she did, Mike turned on his heels, lurched to the side of the car in three or four lunging steps, and punched the window next to Annick's head.

"Jesus!" she screamed, and Mike's fist rocked the tempered glass again, first leaving nothing, then a fracture like breaking ice in a cartoon, then his fist again, bloody this time, leaving the window a soft spiderweb.

"I'm going," said Philip, to himself and to Annick, and as he turned to get out of the car, Mike stopped punching, reached into the waistband of his pants, and pulled out something dull and black.

Annick opened her door and slammed it into his arm, but Mike held onto the gun, and squeezed a loud round off into the air. Annick jaw's locked shut as she pulled the handle back and pushed it out again sharply, quickly, hitting the heel of Mike's hand with the corner of the door and finally loosening his grip. As Mike turned with his bleeding hand to pick up the gun, Philip was on him, knees between his shoulders, punching the back of his neck.

"What are you doing?" someone screamed, and Annick stood to see Lina, still wearing what looked like the shorts she must wear at work, but with a large grey cotton hoodie overtop. "Why don't you leave me alone? Just leave me the fuck alone!"

"Lina, I spend almost all day, almost every day, talking to people who can barely breathe, they feel so guilty. Even though they haven't done anything wrong."

"Just go away, okay? Just go away!"

"You don't need to be afraid to talk to me, Lina. You haven't done anything wrong. But you also know Sanjay Desai didn't kill your boyfriend," Annick said, trying hard to stay calm. Seeing that Philip had neutralized Mike, she stepped out around their bodies and towards Lina, who began shaking her head incoherently.

"I don't. I don't know anything."

"Lina, I want you to relax," Annick said in the same voice she'd used a thousand times in her office, a voice that established authority, safety, calm. "I know you didn't kill Jason. But you can't let someone you know also didn't do it go to prison. Because that's another life. And if you let that happen, then Lina? You *will* have something to feel guilty about. You *will* have taken a life. And for a normal person—a good person, Lina, like you? That kind of guilt will never go away."

Lina began to cry, wet glitter running down both sides of her face.

"They've got—they're very scary people," she said. "And Lewis takes care of his family. I've seen it."

"Lina, I will do everything that I can to help you get out from under that fucking scumbag. Nothing would make me happier."

Lina laughed through the sob. "You can't."

"But there are other people who are going to be hurt from this. There's an innocent young man in jail." Lina wiped her hand roughly across her cheek, the motion saving her from conceding a nod. Annick pushed: "You didn't kill Jason, but I also know that you know who did. You were there when it happened, weren't you?"

"Don't you get it? If I say anything—"

Philip stood with his foot in the middle of Mike's back, pulling a cellphone out of his pocket and beginning to dial.

"Who's he calling?" asked Lina, in a panic.

"He's calling the police."

"No!"

"Lina, I need you to relax."

"Don't call the cops, please."

"The police are going to come and arrest Mike for assault, probably a gun charge. You haven't done anything. They aren't coming for you."

"But Lewis..."

"Listen, I—I think we can do this in a way so that it doesn't come back on you, okay Lina? As far as the cops are concerned, as far as Lewis Blair is concerned. It'll be on me, and I can take care of myself. But before the police get here, I need you to confirm a few things for me. I need to know that I'm right about what happened, so that I can point them in the right direction."

Lina stared at her, stared at Mike.

"Mike is sleeping right now, Lina," Annick explained, and she could hear Philip explaining their location to the emergency dispatcher. "This is just between you and me. I take confidentiality very seriously, Lina. But we don't have a lot of time. So I'm going to ask you to confirm some things I think I already know, okay? Can you do that for me? Can you do that for Jason?"

Lina stared at Annick, and seemed suddenly like a child who had gotten into her mother's makeup. What could she be, twenty-one? Twenty-two? She would have been too young for all of this at any age.

"Okay," she said, shakily.

"Okay. Now, I'm guessing, Lina, that if the police take that blood on my window there, from where Mike punched it, I'm guessing that if they take a look at that blood, it's going to match the blood they found in Jason's room. Am I right to think that?"

Lina nodded.

25

TERRY CHU DRANK black espresso and, at the very least,
Annick could respect him for that. She watched him leaving
Caffé Puglia holding a tiny paper shot, gripping a wax-
paper bag as he walked towards where she was sitting in
the sun. Annick had found a bench next to a soaring glass
wall, slanted at a severe and inorganic angle appropriate to
the sober and austere spirit of the law. After nodding a hello,
Terry sat and began picking the berries out of his scone, and
Annick took a moment to remind herself that mental well-
ness was a broad spectrum.

"Thank you for meeting me," she began. "Especially on
a court day."

"Listen, before you say anything, I'd like to apologize
again. The way I spoke to you the other day, that wasn't fair.
This has been a frustrating case, and until very recently it
didn't feel like my client was levelling with me. Now I know
he wasn't—and I guess, at this point, I understand why. You
helped a lot by reaching out to him."

"Thanks."

"So—are we cool?"

"On the condition that you explain this berry thing."

"What, this? I like the flavour that berries give a scone,
but I can't stand the texture of any fruit that has been heated."

"I respect a man who knows what he wants in a baked good."

"Life's too short, you know? So tell me about this good news. I could use it."

"Are you with Sanjay today?"

"Later. This is something else, a burglary charge." Terry grimaced a lost-cause smile. "They found my guy with his dead father's whole collection of sculptures and paintings, all crammed into his condo storage locker, before the executor had even had a chance to read the will. So fucked up. He's got all these brothers and sisters, they sit in the courtroom, they're practically hissing at him."

"You like an underdog, huh?"

"Karmically, I figure I'm building up one hell of an IOU from the universe. Which your text last night kind of made it sound like you might be delivering?"

Annick smiled. "The girl, the dancer?"

A look of excitement passed across Terry's face, lifting him up from his work with the berries. "Yeah?"

"She didn't do it."

"I thought you said this was good news?"

"She knows who did it, though."

"Can she prove it?"

"You don't want to know who?"

"Doesn't matter who if she can't prove it."

"Man, you really are a lawyer."

"What can I say? I imagine you're the same way about psychology."

"Good guess. But she doesn't have to prove anything."

"Okay?"

Two lawyers in full colonial costume passed by, smiling to each other conspiratorially as one quietly explained something infinitely exciting to the other, and Terry's eyes raised to follow them just for a moment before returning to Annick.

"Mike Collis."

"The guy's best friend? The thickneck that wrote the Facebook post?"

"The very same."

"No!" Terry said, staring into the middle distance. "The balls on that guy." Then, after another pause: "What a fucking asshole!"

"Hiding in plain sight."

"So first tell me what happened, then how we can prove it."

"Jason and Lina were apparently always fighting—even I knew that, before this whole thing exploded. To hear her tell it, they were head over heels in love, but it's a difficult piece of psychology to manage, working security at the same club where drunk dipshits ogle your girlfriend on stage, and big-time players in the VIP lounge, guys you could never stand up to or they'd put you in the ground, take even greater liberties."

"Woah," said Terrence, pie-eyed, and Annick could sense that not all of his interest in the story was strictly down to legal strategy.

"Jason was a jealous type, and from what I'm told, they would go back and forth about her work, arguing about it, then reconciling with just as much heat."

Staring at Annick, Terry absent-mindedly fed one of the baked berries off of his scone into his mouth, curling his face up in disgust and spitting it onto the ground.

"So, what? There's a confrontation at the house? Jason, operating as a standard-issue dirtbag jealous boyfriend, tried to kill Mike—that gives us the extra blood—and then Mike gets him back in self-defence?"

"Not exactly. Apparently, Mike, who has delusions of climbing the ladder in his uncle's organization—"

"Who's his uncle?"

"Lewis Blair."

"Jesus Christ!" Terry shouted, expanding himself, hands spreading wide, knees flying open, knocking his briefcase over and upsetting its contents. A few yards away, a swarm of television journalists was closing in on an attorney and her high-profile client, and an eruption of laughter met a line delivered by one or the other of them just as the scrum began; across from them, a group in late adolescence was trying to climb the concrete benches with their skateboards. But the more that seemed to be going on outside of the court-houses, the tighter the focus of Terry Chu's concentration. When she saw that he wasn't moving to refill his open brief-case, Annick pressed on.

"Apparently Mike had been throwing his weight around in the VIP room, trying to show off for some of the high rollers. Then, asserting whatever the strip club slash brothel version of droit de seigneur is, he manhandled Lina in front of them. Jason pulled him off her, in front of everybody, shoved him over a side table covered in drinks. Apparently Mike looked like one of the Stooges, completely humiliated."

"Emasculated."

"Sure, if that helps."

"So he killed him."

Annick nodded. "She was there, but I promised her that in our version, she wouldn't be."

"But I'll need her."

Annick shook her head. "No, you won't. The blood, the extra blood? It's his. Mike burst in on the two of them—"

"Remind me to get the brand name of Sanjay's headphones."

"No shit, right? It didn't help that he likes his music loud."

"Kids think they're invincible. That they'll never go deaf."

"So while Sanjay's off in sensory-deprivation land, Mike comes over to the house, he's upset, he wants to talk to Jason and Lina. Jason sends Lina to the bedroom, so the boys can lock antlers in the living room or the kitchen, and after a few minutes, Mike storms out, and Jason goes back to the room with Lina. But almost as quickly as he leaves, Mike's back, into the bedroom now by way of the kitchen, lunging at Jason with the knife, screaming about how he made a fool of him in front of these big guys. But Mike can't fight for shit—I can attest to that myself, I've seen it twice now. So even though he makes a big show, Jason gets the knife off of him, slashes his arm. Now, Lina says, Mike starts whimpering, and Jason throws the knife on the floor because he thinks it's over, his friend is calming down. But he isn't—instead, Mike grabs Lina's shoulders, flings her to the ground. She falls onto her back, and when Jason bolts over to check on her, that's when Mike picks the knife back up, opens Jason's throat from behind."

"Holy shit."

"He grabs the knife—"

"Hence no murder weapon..."

"—and he grabs Lina hard by the wrist, covers her mouth because she's losing it. He hears Sanjay go into the bathroom, hears the water start running, and she says Mike whispered that he had to kill Sanjay, too, but she bit the inside of his hand and he barrelled them outside and into his car. She says later, Mike's going out of his mind, swinging between screaming rage and just bawling like a baby. A few hours later, when they see the first story online that the cops have arrested Sanjay, Mike says how Jason told him about Sanjay's OCD before, his complaints to the landlords. Even a mug as dumb as Mike could see that he had a scapegoat."

"And she doesn't say anything until now, because?"

"Fuck-up that he is, Mike's still Lewis Blair's nephew. She's still terrified. That's why we can't have her there, on the scene."

Terry shook his head. "Nope. I'm sorry, I do—I need a reason to take his blood."

Annick smiled. "No, you don't. Because right before Mike Collis was arrested last night for assault and possession of an illegal firearm—"

"Wait, what? How do you know this?"

"—he punched a blood sample right into the window of the car I was driving."

Terry Chu sat in dumbfounded silence for a few seconds, then spread his moustache over a wide, full-face smile. "Hells yes. Holy shit. Dr. Boudreau, I misjudged you."

"Could've happened to anyone."

"The balls, I still can't believe it. That Facebook post."

"The guy's an asshole. But he didn't do it alone—he has every dumbshit on the internet to thank. So, here's what I need you to do, while they still have him in custody."

"Shoot."

"You tell the swaggering VPD sergeant, what's his name?"

"Bremner."

"You tell Sergeant Bremner the version of the story where Lina's on the other side of town. If he has any problem with her absence, shift the conversation to the fact that you're helping me prepare a formal complaint to the Human Rights Tribunal that the police department acted in a way that was prejudicial to my patient on the basis of his mental health."

Terry laughed. "He'll flip out. They just settled with the family of that guy, the schizophrenic they tasered into a coma on Robson Street."

"Throw in Supriya's poetry, the anti-brutality stuff."

"That's considerate of you."

"I'm feeling magnanimous. We good?"

"Yes, Dr. Boudreau. We're very good."

Annick stood and extended a hand, but Terry leaned in to a deeply genuine hug, and she was happy to reciprocate.

"Can I ask one thing?" he said.

"Sure."

"How come you're not afraid of Lewis Blair?"

Annick raised her palms slightly. "Who said I'm not afraid of Lewis Blair?"

"I see," said Terry.

"But it's like I always tell my patients," Annick said, already moving. "You can't control every variable, every possible bad outcome. You could die crossing the street, but that doesn't mean you stop doing it. Lewis Blair shows up, I don't know. I can take care of myself, I guess."

"Yeah, sounds like," Terry said, turning back to his berryless scone, gathering his fallen pens and pencils with the tip of a brown leather shoe.

~

*"Dr. Manley, this really does feel like a stunning turn of events. After becoming an anti-*PC *hero online, Michael Collis has now been charged with the very murder of which he accused Sanjay Desai. Do you and other mental health-care professionals feel vindicated? Is this a learning moment for Canada?"*

"Well, Sam, I'm a Buddhist, and not to put too fine a point on it, but I believe that every in-breath and every out-breath are potential learning moments."

Annick rolled her eyes so hard she thought she might lose them.

"Nevertheless, we're all familiar, even those with no mental health training whatsoever, with the phenomenon of projection. Too many of us have come to cope with our own deep-seated anxieties about ourselves, about our own worthiness or unworthiness of love, by imagining all of our own faults exaggerated in the countenances of others. So for young Michael Collis to take to social media in such a cruel and foolish way, to denounce young Mr. Desai for the very crime which he, allegedly, committed, strikes me simply as an exaggerated version of what so many of us do nearly every day. When Mr. Collis eventually goes to trial, he may well do so as the first defendant in history to plead someone else's insanity."

"Thank you, Dr. Manley. You've been listening to Dr. Cedric Manley of the West Coast Cognitive Behavioural Therapy Clinic here on 604 at Six. My thanks to Dr. Manley. I'm Sam Gill filling in for Roxanne Tremblay and we'll be right back after your hourly news break, when Kevin Sartorelli will tell us what we can expect from our Canucks in the coming NHL season..."

Cedric really did have a perfectly mellifluous voice, Annick thought as she parked a block from the Jerusalem Artichoke, opened the driver's side door and staggered towards the restaurant. She was running on fumes now, not an hour's good sleep behind her for days, but Arwa would have a grainy pot of cardamom-scented Turkish coffee for her; the silty, strong stuff, the caffeine fiend's equivalent of freebasing.

Even before the coffee, though, she was shot through with a joyous wakefulness by the sight of Sanjay, sitting next to his mother, greyish and timid but free, now, and smiling subtly from the corner of his mouth at something that Supriya was saying. The sight of them blurred behind a wall of tears, but through it Annick saw the impression of her patient rising from his seat, running to her, and she threw her arms around him. Supriya stood and smiled, not even trying not to cry, not even wiping the tears that were streaming down her cheeks.

"Okay, sweetie," Annick said. "If I stay in this hug any longer it's an ethical breach."

Sanjay smiled, fully this time, and sat down at the table.

"They brought us hummus and eggplant to start," Sanjay said, and Annick couldn't stop smiling at him, proud of him for some reason, beaming with affection.

"Thank you, Sanjay."

"*Marhaba*, Annick!" said Mahmoud, leaning in for a hug.

"*Bonsoir*, Mahmoud."

"And good, you brought back your beautiful friend."

"Yes," said Annick, "and a very hungry young man. Eh?"

"Yes," said Sanjay, smiling boyishly, and Supriya laid her hand on the back of his neck, and kissed his cheek.

"Very good, very good."

"You know, Mahmoud," Annick said, spotting an opening. "Supriya here is also an artist."

"Really?"

"Well, yes," Supriya answered with smiling reticence. "A poet."

Mahmoud clutched his chest. "Ah, poetry. This is the true Palestinian religion. Not Islam, not Christianity—poetry! Did you know I am named after a poet?"

"Mahmoud Darwish?" guessed Supriya. Mahmoud made the same face he would have if she'd presented him with a massive novelty cheque.

"Yes! You know Mahmoud Darwish? Oh, my God—beautiful and cultured, your friends, Annick! Come," he said, reaching out his hand to Supriya. "I want to show you my new pieces, can I?"

"Yes, sure," Supriya said, rising, then turning to the table. "Are you two okay?"

"Yes, Mom."

"We're great. Go see the artwork."

"Yes, they are fine, come, tell me your favourite poem by Darwish..."

Annick grinned as she watched them on their way to the back of the restaurant, and happily ran a finger through her missing hair. Arwa touched her warmly on the shoulder as she put down the pot of Turkish coffee, and Annick poured tiny cups for herself and for Sanjay.

"I was hoping we might get a chance to talk one-on-one for a second," she said.

"Yeah," said Sanjay. "Me too."

"How are you doing?" She asked it in a way that he knew it was a real question, not small-talk detritus. Sanjay shrugged.

"I mean, relatively? I'm thrilled. It's—I don't really know how to say it, like, how much better it is to be back home now, to be in my own clothes. But the thoughts?"

"Yeah?"

"The thoughts have been really bad. And I'm scared, like—all the people, who saw that post about me..." Thick, wet tears dropped out of Sanjay's large brown eyes. "The worst part of it all was how scary it all was, and, I don't know—it's, like, fucked up and everything, but even though I'm out, I don't know. I feel just as scared."

Annick nodded. She reached a hand across the table to Sanjay, grabbed his fingers and squeezed.

"This has been a trauma, Sanjay. They catch the real bad guy, that's only the end in the movies. It's the end of your legal troubles, but the mental and emotional toll of this experience? Taking care of that is going to take a lot of work."

"Yeah," Sanjay managed through his tears. "I know. Okay."

"Okay?"

"Yes," he sniffed.

"You know I'm a psychologist, not a psychiatrist—I'm agnostic when it comes to meds. But it may be worth talking to your GP about something to at least have on hand, Clonazepam, Ativan, something along those lines just for the panic over the next few months."

"Yeah."

"You've heard of post-traumatic stress, right? Nobody could go through what you've just endured without coming away shaken. You're not going to shrug this off, and no one should expect you to. You come by what you're feeling very, very honestly, Sanjay."

He smiled weakly, nodding his head.

"And listen, if given what we've been through over the past week or so, you feel like you want to proceed with a different psychologist—"

"What?" he asked, in a startled panic. "Did I do something wrong?"

"What? No, Sanjay. Not even a little bit. But some people might feel like this... experience we just went through together—if it changed the therapeutic dynamic between us, involved me too much in your personal life—"

"All you did was help me! Before, and then during this whole thing. I just—I don't want another doctor. I feel safe with you. Please don't make me see somebody else. Please, Dr. Boudreau?"

Annick did her best to still the trembling in her lower lip. "Of course, Sanjay," she said. "Of course. I'm going to be heading back East for the next couple of weeks, my dad just got out of surgery—"

"Oh, I'm sorry."

"That's okay. Thank you. I just mention it so that you know that, for the next little bit, I won't be around. But I'm going to leave you with my cell number, my email, and if you need anything, Sanjay, at any time—I want you to reach out to me, okay?"

"Okay."

"I'm really proud of you, Sanjay."

"Why?"

"You're here."

As Mahmoud returned to the table, he was smiling broadly, the crook of Supriya's elbow resting in his hand.

"Okay! Okay, it's decided, we're going to work together," Mahmoud announced triumphantly as they returned to the table. "Your beautiful friend Supriya is going to supply the text, and me the photographs. It's going to be amazing." Supriya smiled shyly, sitting down.

"I'll do my best."

"Oh, you don't have a choice, a true artist always does their best. Same with the psychologist. Same with Arwa, tonight, she gonna make you the most beautiful—lamb, chicken, you ever had a Palestinian dumpling?"

"Only you, Mahmoud," Annick said. He slapped her hand with the floppy, laminated menu.

"My wife hears you, I'm in the street, that's it!"

"Okay, I'll keep it down."

"Let us prepare the meal for you, okay? No menus."

"No menus."

"No menus."

"Yeah, okay. No menus."

"Good!" Mahmoud took off at close to a run, back to the kitchen, and Supriya turned back to Annick.

"He's a character."

"He's the best."

"Dr. Boudreau, this Saturday evening we're going to have a little party at our home, a welcome back party, and it would mean so much to us if you would join us."

"No, Mom—she's going out of town."

"Oh?"

"Yeah, my father's just got out of surgery—"

"Oh no!"

"—in Halifax, yeah. So I'm going to be with him. But to be honest with you, Supriya, I think I would've had to respectfully decline, anyway."

"Really? Why?"

Annick turned to Sanjay, smiled, reached and squeezed his hand one more time.

"Because Sanjay already has friends. I'm his doctor."

~

"You sure you're gonna be okay?"

"I will, baby. Thank you."

"Because if you need me, I just need a few days to swing it and I can hop on a plane. You can explain to everybody in Halifax what an Asian person is."

"Why would I ever share the secret to my happiness?"

Annick leaned over and kissed Philip for longer than he was allowed to stop the car in front of the airport.

"You give 'Méo a big hug for me, okay? Tell him I still expect that moose hunt."

"I will."

"You should sleep."

"How long have you known me? When have I ever fallen asleep on a plane?"

"I know, but—it's been a crazy couple weeks. If you can rest, do it."

"I'll have plenty of time to sleep when you're on that moose-hunting trip."

"Alright, alright. Fly safe, baby."

"It's not up to me." She gave him one more kiss, then took her rolling carry-on from the small car-share trunk. "*Je t'aime, mon amour.*"

"Me too."

Annick felt her shoulders relaxing in the security lineup, just as everyone else's were tensing up. She lifted her small suitcase into the large plastic tray, pre-emptively removed her sneakers and quietly celebrated the fact that her merino leggings didn't have pockets to empty.

It was a long way to the Atlantic Ocean, but in something close to a miracle, she'd found a non-stop flight, and she'd brought a book, a popular history of Louisiana, that she had promised her father months ago that she would read, so that they could plan a family trip to visit the far-flung Boudreaus of bayou country.

She boarded shamelessly into business class, stowed her case with dignity and attached her seat belt, laying out a rough plan for the flight. The coffee at this end of the plane ride would be passable, and given two movies and a healthy chunk of reading about the expulsion and resettlement of her ancestors, she'd be there. Relatively painless.

But as the plane slipped up through the low clouds over the Fraser River, the wheels retracting loudly into the body of the craft after takeoff, the seat belt sign still illuminated, in the second row window seat of business class, Dr. Annick Boudreau was fast asleep.

Author's Note & Acknowledgements

G.K. CHESTERTON BASED his most beloved detective, Father Brown, on the man who had saved his soul; I have similarly based my detective on the person who saved my mind (besides an expansive waistline, that's more or less all I have in common with Chesterton; he was a much better writer than I'll ever be, and I have way, way better politics). Nevertheless, the moment she appeared on the page, Dr. Annick Boudreau became her own, *made-up* person—and though she shares the traits of kindness, professionalism and commitment with her inspiration, she is entirely fictional.

The German film about the Stasi that Annick and Philip had watched was the brilliant *The Lives of Others* (2006). The non-fiction of Daniel Francis and Jerry Langton provided indirect inspiration for some of the Vancouver underworld elements of the story—though all characters are of my own creation and wholly imaginary. The Jerusalem Artichoke, and its owners, Arwa and Mahmoud, are, sadly, also make-believe—but the good news is that the food is even better at the very real Tamam Fine Palestinian Cuisine in the East Vancouver neighbourhood of Hastings-Sunrise.

Though poetic licence was taken with the descriptions of my therapist-detective, no such liberties were taken with the depiction of the symptoms of primary obsessions OCD; it's exactly as painful and pernicious as I've laid it out, and my knowledge of it is very hard-won, not through research but from experience. If you are experiencing these sorts of intrusive thoughts, let me only tell you two things: first, you have not done anything wrong, and there is nothing wrong with you but an overactive sense of moral obligation and a series of errors of interpretation. The only victim of these thoughts is you. Whatever thoughts you're having, I promise you: mine were worse. Which leads me to the second thing: with help, you can get a handle on OCD, essentially defeating it, and life will turn into something so much better you could scarcely imagine it. Talk to someone you trust, a medical or therapeutic professional, family or friend. If you live in one of the too-common jurisdictions where psychological or psychiatric treatment is not state-provided and falls outside of your financial capability, a good place to start is with the book *Overcoming Obsessive Thoughts: How to Gain Control of Your OCD* by David A. Clark and Christine Purdon. Thank you to Tejpal Singh Swatch, the first person to whom I was able to admit my own OCD; thank you to Stephen Hui, who steered me towards cognitive behavioural therapy; and thank you to all of the family, friends and medical practitioners who have helped me to fight an illness that I once thought would make life not worth living.

This story takes place in a city that I adore, that has always been my home—I gratefully acknowledge the Squamish, Musqueam and Tsleil-Waututh nations, whose unceded territories Vancouver was built upon, and—hopefully, as we start to make amends—alongside.

Thank you to Dr. Lee Trentadue and Dr. James Schmidt, along with my own therapist (who, like many great heroes, will remain anonymous), for answering procedural and professional questions about the work, ethics and responsibilities of psychologists. *Grosses bises à Mamie, ma grandmère Alberte Boudreau.* My pal Sam Wiebe was an invaluable help and source of encouragement, and I'm grateful both for his work and for his friendship, as I am grateful for bosom buddy Rob Simmons, whose counsel over duck confit at The Argo will always be sought and appreciated. Thanks to my agent, John Pearce, and to Chris Casuccio, at Westwood Creative Artists; thanks to Anna Comfort O'Keeffe, Brianna Cerkiewicz and everyone at Douglas & McIntyre, with whom I have always loved working; profoundest gratitude for Caroline Skelton, whose patience and editorial skill made for a much better novel than what could have been; thank you to copy editor Nicola Goshulak, the only person on earth whom I'm willing to admit knows the geography of Vancouver better than I do, and to proofreader Lucy Kenward. Thank you to Zoe Grams and Ariel Hudnall at ZG Communications—if you heard about this book, it's likely thanks to them.

Thank you to my mystery-loving mother-in-law, Pauline Tong, especially for making possible the two very brightest lights in my life, my wife, Cara Ng, and my daughter, Joséphine Ng-Demers.

And, to Cara: whatever the diagnosis is, caring for an ill spouse takes a grace and selflessness that I hope I could, but will never have to, match in return. I could not be more grateful to have you beside me. *Je t'aime.*

About the Author

CHARLES DEMERS IS an author, comedian, actor, playwright, screenwriter and political activist. His collection of essays, *Vancouver Special* (Arsenal Pulp Press, 2009), was shortlisted for the Hubert Evans BC Book Prize for Non-Fiction. He is also the author of a novel, *The Prescription Errors* (Insomniac Press, 2009). He is one of the most frequently returning stars of CBC Radio's smash-hit comedy *The Debaters*, with a weekly listening audience of 750,000. Demers lives in Vancouver, BC, where he is working on a second book in the Dr. Boudreau Mystery series, *Suicidal Thoughts*.